ANTHONY MARAIS

The Cure

BALNEUM BOOKS

FIRST EDITION

Cover design by the author
Prepress by Bernd Zemanek

Published by BALNEUM BOOKS
P.O. Box 9082 Newport Beach, CA 92658
email: balneumbooks@aol.com

Printed and bound in the Czech Republic

Front cover: 19th century French engraving
of the Kochbrunnen in Wiesbaden, Germany

Back cover: "The Seventh Key" from The Golden Tripod,
Francfort-on-the-Main, 1618

Visit our website at **www.anthonymarais.com**

ISBN 0-9774792-0-X

*One thing at least is certain: water and madness have long been linked in the
dreams of European man.*

Michel Foucault (Madness and Civilization)

Contents

PART ONE

Nigredo

Chapter I

Robert woke up in a cold sweat. He hadn't been sleeping well lately—this was the third night in a row without two consecutive hours of slumber—however, until now, none of his dreams had so abruptly startled him out of rest. Hardly had he opened his eyes when the details began to dissipate into subconsciousness, although certain images remained in mind. He was in a large house, one with no windows, containing a long hallway and many rooms; each room had a different sized door, some of them were cracked, emitting an orange glow, some were wide open, and still others were bolted shut with paper stuffed in the keyholes. He could vaguely recall the voice of a haggard old lady, calling forth the passerby (it had just occurred to him that there were other shadowy forms alongside him); and when he approached her, she seized him and forced him into one of the rooms.

There was no memory of the door being shut, however, as if in a film, he was suddenly locked in. Lying on the bed, crouched like an animal, was a woman, shivering and naked. Robert approached her and began to caress her body, fingering her legs and then for a long time pressing the upper part of her thighs at which point she took him into her arms, clinging to him in a particularly unpleasant manner. He tried to push her away, but her limbs stuck to him like tentacles. Suddenly he was running along a beach, his feet sticking to the sand, and just as quickly there was a dog attacking him, viciously gnawing his leg, and then this beast and his body were melting together at which point he screamed and woke up.

For a moment he was at a loss as to his whereabouts. Last thing he remembered he had been in Berkeley, before that Vancouver. Now he was here, in this place called Wiesbaden. Friends of the family had a flat in a nice part of town, enabling him to use a guestroom in the attic. Back home he had the chance to work, a job that could have very well solved his problems, but a little money remained from a student loan and for some reason a trip to Europe seemed better. He lifted his head and rubbed some sleep from his eyes. The best thing to do is take a walk, he thought, propping himself up on one elbow and pushing his pillow aside. None of the stress that had been taxing him until now was going to disappear with a few extra hours of sleep. The best thing to do is move, he kept telling himself, over and over in his mind until he no longer realized that he was dreaming again.

Upon reawakening, he found his resolve considerably weakened. He had no reason to get up, and for once he wasn't going to pretend he did. After all, in spite of some luck in getting here, things couldn't have possibly been worse. He was a university dropout. It felt like a dream when it happened: walking into the department and explaining to the secretary that he would be leaving indefinitely. She was aware of his struggles, but was surprised all the same when he gave the news. She liked Robert, and throughout the scandal (whereby he decided to accuse his supervisor of plagiarism) she had been on his side. A lot of people liked Robert. Nevertheless, when his conflict reached the dean's office, and thus became public, he noticed a subtle distance had grown between himself and everyone around him. Perhaps they were all on his side, but no one showed it.

He rolled over and buried his face in his pillow. Stubbornly, he tried to reenter the dream he had just had. He pictured himself in his supervisor's office talking wildly in a state of excitement as a hundred arguments came rushing out of him, all with the aim of convincing himself the problem could be resolved. A mere three months ago he was the pride of his family, undergrads were tripping over themselves to meet him, and professors were inviting him to dinner. He had studied hard and gone far quickly towards a successful career in archaeology. He had visions of being the person with the answers to heal all wounds. Now he was nothing. It may as well have been stamped on his forehead: he was a coward and his only success was in fleeing.

Chapter II

He must have eaten something bad or, perhaps, had spent too much time walking around in the cold, because it was getting on dark and Robert still had a headache. He reached for his backpack and pulled out a box of aspirin; then he called over the waitress and ordered a glass of mineral water. After popping two tablets he took a large swig, swished the chalky mixture a bit, gargled, and then swallowed it down in a single gulp.

Germany: a country where until recently Robert had never before set foot nor given a second thought. In misguided kindness, he had been warned about the people with whom he was dealing, entering a world of order where overt friendliness and public extroversion were not to be found—but this didn't bother him. He had not intended to take the journey seriously or to commit himself deeply to it, but simply to wind down after a year of stress. Lately, perhaps in response to this stress, Robert had started reading novels, essays and poems (if he had been paying better attention, this should have raised concern); and subsequently, for the first time in his twenty-nine years, he discovered in himself something which he had always possessed, but recently lost: a soul.

And yet what does this word mean? Apparently, as far as he could understand what he was reading, a soul was that delicate essence that constitutes who we really are and retreats every time an academic enters the room. Some readers may find this difficult to believe, but Robert (by no means a dull kid) made it through childhood without having read much. His high school years were spent trying to forget what little he had learned in grade school; and by the time he entered college, and later university, science had crept into the picture before art ever had a chance to blossom (reading became that which is found in a reader). But something in him must have yearned for that recondite domain, for he ended up studying anthropology: that peculiar faculty which attempts to ascertain man (chaos) in the realm of science (order)—in other words, it's the soup kitchen for those who can't decide whether a tiki is a god or carved stone. During the last year of his studies—a year quite literally monopolized by the "culture wars" which arose out of the impact of structuralism, and more particularly post-structuralism—order was on the rise (the tiki was looking ever more like carved stone), and from out of nowhere chaos made its attack; and, not insignificantly, literature was at the front.

Now seated across the room was a group of women, giggling and looking at some photos, the most attractive of which was sitting legs crossed in a large wicker chair with awning, lending her the mien of a Hollywood star lounging at poolside. Robert found himself staring, but when she caught him he looked away. He felt the urge to smile to her, but his self-restraint abided and he retreated to his drink, peering into it until she no longer had a reason to take an interest in him. And yet there was a compelling allure behind her goldilocks façade. Here was a stunning woman who looked neither overly made up, nor underdressed—suddenly she looked at him again, this time directly in the eyes, and smiled. Robert, out of instinct, returned the gesture, but he couldn't withstand the waiting, the commitment to act, to say something when exchanging a look with someone longer than the accepted length of a glance. He turned away again.

After a while the women began to collect their things and go. The blonde smiled, took her handbag and was the last of her friends to leave. Just then an old man at the bar in a loud voice said something Robert couldn't understand. The bartender laughed. Admittedly, this sort of "innocent" flirtation never ceased to cause Robert angst. The reasons for this guilt were deep-seated and manifold; however, it was mainly due to the fact he had a girlfriend waiting for him back home. He imagined that at that moment she was trifling with a man in some café. In all probability she smiled back to her courtier, swapped a few words with the guy, and cheerfully went on her way, chaste as a girl in Sunday school. Robert, on the other hand, now found himself dreaming of the "Hollywood Star," acting out in his mind innumerable scenarios of what he should have done and what might have been.

Chapter III

The Café Laumer, like the rest of Frankfurt, is inconspicuous, not particularly attractive, but has a colorful history. In the 1920s, it served as meeting point for the sociologists of the renowned Frankfurt Institute of Social Research, until they were forced to emigrate in 1933. During the protests of 1968, it was the location of a pie and cake fight between the hippies and the establishment. Today, the place looks more suited to relaxation than to revolution, the only visible sign of its intellectual past being found on the breakfast menu, which has named the meals after academic disciplines. Robert had some business to take care of at the U.S. Consulate (his visa wouldn't last till Christmas) and thought it a good chance to visit Jürgen who worked nearby.

Robert had recently met Jürgen at the Café Parsival (the place with attractive women) and decided to take him up on an offer for coffee. Jürgen had studied law in Leipzig, and was now working in Frankfurt and living with his girlfriend in Wiesbaden. To Robert he seemed to be one of those rare cases who traipsed through life without the slightest hesitation. Life was too short to worry, he had explained at their last meeting, and people who fuss over it are dumb. This was his style; and that was that.

Moreover, one had the impression that Jürgen struggled with every word—not because he was speaking a foreign language, but because he had racked himself with the task to never beat around the bush. For him, Wiesbaden was a place like any other, and if he had chosen to live in Berlin or Munich, he would have surely met someone like Robert there, and they would have had similar conversations. He admitted, however, that this town had a strange affect on his sense of time. People around here just don't respect it, he said. They plan their vacations as if the six months in between didn't count, they buy their bus passes by the year, and twenty-five-year-olds discuss retirement options. The idea of seizing the day never took root; the week was the minimum unit.

Robert took a seat near the window and looked out onto the street. It was as if someone had made a conscious effort at defying any form or design that would in the least way suggest personality; apartment houses were unanimously smeared with the same white stucco, windows all had the same white framework and all the details, like gates and benches and lampposts, which so ornately enhance other cities, here were devoid of frill—the whole neighborhood presented itself as a monotonous blocky expanse, providing the eye with nothing to lock onto except for a few glassy buildings popping out above the rooftops. "This is the home of the hot dog?" Robert thought, glancing at a yellow phone booth that looked as if it were stolen from Legoland. There was simply nothing to offer a point of reference to the vision one conjures up when imagining the fairy tale land of the brothers Grimm, or the horse-and-carriage world of Goethe (who was, after all, originally from Frankfurt).

Then, breaking Robert's gaze, and yet somehow in harmony with this landscape, Jürgen came sauntering up the street. Robert was thankful they had met, and it showed when he waved hello. The two shook hands, Jürgen took a seat and, without warning, burst into conversation: "You know," he declared, running his fingers through his fine blond hair, "Americans can be nice, but they don't know how to speak. You know what I mean? Spit out the chewing gum! And the worst is when they call me 'Gergin' instead of 'Yoorgen'."

The fiery German thrust his English about like a barbarian his sword; that is to say awkwardly, with a heavy accent, but effectively. Robert, unperturbed by the attack—on the contrary, enjoying Jürgen's bombastic nature—countered with the obvious question: "Then why do you like America so much?"

"Like it?" he asked, curling his lips into a ball. "What do you mean? I hate it! All the problems of the world come from America! Fat people come from America! Loud people! Dumb Hollywood films! Thin books! Silicon breasts, superficiality and war!"

Jürgen had a way of saying all he had to say on any particular subject in a single flash, no matter what his frame of mind, so that it was very easy for people to discover with whom they were dealing. Robert, opting to keep his cool, tactfully parried his friend's jab and simply reminded him that he had been there seven times. Thereupon Jürgen began to twitch and tremble like a volcano on the verge of eruption, but then, as if a ray of happiness broke through his storm, a smile appeared on his usually earnest face. "Yes," he conceded, "and I go back in May."

The two shared a good laugh and Jürgen grabbed a menu, perusing the choices and complaining that none of it sounded edible. As far as he was concerned, philosophers didn't eat breakfast. Robert was nonetheless taken with the café. He was also thinking that Jürgen wore funny glasses: with round wire rims and a squiggle along the side that reached back to the ear without bending around it, like a design student's thesis project, overly serious and futuristic to a fault. With his blond hair, blue eyes and rugged cheekbones he would have been a handsome guy had it not been for his big ears.

"By the way," he said without looking from his menu, "are you coming to our New Year's Eve party?"

"Um, yea sure," Robert answered, counting his fingers, "but that's still a long way off. I mean, it's not even November yet."

"Naturally it's a long way off," asserted Jürgen, tossing the menu on the table and crossing his legs, "but we must plan it in advance! It's the highpoint of the year and I don't want you to plan anything else. Do you understand? You must come! Naturally, you know that in Germany we shoot fireworks. Oh, it's good fun, and you won't go home hungry."

"Of course, that sounds great," Robert smiled, "but, you know, I really can't tell you where I'll be in two months. I mean, I'm living day to day right now, and"—it was evident that Jürgen wasn't going to take no for an answer—"and…well I can promise you this: no matter what, if I'm still in Germany on December 31st, I'll go to your party. Okay? I swear it."

Jürgen, satisfied with the verbal agreement he had coerced from his friend, called the waitress over and ordered; but just as she was leaving the table, Jürgen put his hand on Robert's shoulder, gave it a firm squeeze, and said: "If I told you that you will die in the next two months, what would you say? You will die in the first days of the New Year."

"Where in the world did that come from?" asked Robert, caught off guard by the sudden and unpleasant prediction.

"A special colleague asked me it at my meeting this week. He said everyone should be able to answer this question."

"Don't you find that a bit morbid? And what do you mean by special colleague? What meeting?"

"I'm serious, tell me. Would you travel? Visit friends? Family?"

Robert began fidgeting on his chair, and then stopped, folded his arms and exhaled loudly through his nostrils. "I don't know. I guess I wouldn't do much."

"What do you mean," Jürgen said, disgruntled, "you wouldn't do much?"

"I don't know," Robert went on, gazing out the window. This guy didn't hear that Californians don't die, he thought, but decided to hold his tongue. Anyway, such questions demand no response. All they do is elicit useless philosophizing and, in the end, waste time and energy. And then, appearing as if the answer had been found, he said: "I'd probably go find a park bench and take a nap."

"That's not possible!" cried Jürgen, nearly bursting a blood vessel in his rage.

As the waitress returned with their food, nervously placing it before Jürgen, Robert was compelled to ask, "Okay, then, what would you do?"

Jürgen pushed his spectacles back on his nose. "Me?" he asked, glancing at his breakfast. "I would take my girlfriend on a tour of America. We could get a Harley, drive out to the middle of the desert, beneath the red hills, surrounded by cactus, and smoke a peace pipe with a crazy old Indian chief. My last moments of life would be spent alone under the stars on a vision quest."

"That sounds great," Robert said, "but, you see, my problem is that I'm already there—I mean here. I've made my trip, and I'm not even dead yet!" Then he looked his friend squarely in the eyes: "Now what?"

"Now what?" Jürgen repeated, freezing and making a face of utmost concentration, as if Robert had touched upon a vitally relevant topic: "Now the photocopies for Dorfmeyer! I almost forgot! I'm sorry, but we must finish this another time. Käfer's would be good; maybe Thursday night."

"Kay—what? I'm sorry I don't understand."

Jürgen didn't answer. He simply got up, stuffed an egg in his mouth, buttoned his coat, reached for his bag, and darted out of the café before the door had swung shut from a customer entering. It wasn't until he was outside breaking into a sprint down the sidewalk that he thought to wave goodbye.

Chapter IV

For the amateur of culture, a language course abroad is a special treat: it's a trove of worldviews from a dozen countries and a bounty of opinions on normally straightforward topics. Robert's class was a mix of Czechs, Poles, Turks, Swedes, Lithuanians, Hungarians, and a Russian from Saint Petersburg. Most were in their early twenties and eager to learn. They were in Germany for its economy, working as au pairs, maids or construction workers, trying to save up some money, hoping to get into university, or simply in need of change. Two notable exceptions were Robert and the woman who sat next to him: a 38-year-old Bosnian history teacher. She also worked as a maid during the day for families who probably thought they were doing her a favor by letting her mop floors.

The course dragged on—from an exercise on prepositions to naming the objects found in a kitchen to an activity whereby students had to hold a card over their heads and guess the word—and Robert found himself repeatedly glancing at his watch. Perhaps (at precisely this point) the reader would like to hear how the teacher discussed his family under Adolf Hitler or how at Auschwitz Rudolf Hoess, collaborating with the I.G. Farben company in Frankfurt, came upon on the idea of using Zyklon B gas, previously used to exterminate rats, as a means of optimizing the Holocaust; but this simply wasn't the case. The subject matter was, for better or for worse, quite banal and held to themes complementary to the petty bourgeois culture of which Germans seem to be so fond (i.e., shopping, sports, cars and the German standard of living).

In any case, on this particular evening the banality was too much to bear, and when the course finally came to an end, no one noticed the hurried pace at which Robert left the building. Once on the street, breathing in the cool air and clasping his hands for warmth, he felt, for a moment, good. He walked a bit further—then stopped. He slowly turned and gazed down the alley he had just entered. He looked to the left, and then to the right. Then he started off again, this time walking with a cautious step.

Several days later Robert found himself again unable to sleep. Although there were many recurring themes lately that brought him out of slumber—or, in the worst cases, refused him even a wink of shuteye—this time it was the university crisis again: It had occurred to him that at the very moment when his troubles were at their worst (when he was trying to deal with both his supervisor and moving out), his best friend had started having problems with his girlfriend and wasn't able to offer a bed in his flat. At the time, Robert was feeling sorry for the guy, and even remembered feeling guilty that he wasn't in a condition to offer much support. But now it dawned on him that this, too, could have been part of the isolation that was encompassing him. The strength that he was showing toward the school was being challenged from literally every side of his life!

Not that it was unexpected. The fact that any display of defiance on the part of a grad student toward his or her supervisor (issues of plagiarism, neglect or sexual harassment) was automatically perceived as an act of opportunism in the eyes of the dean was common knowledge (and what was shunned by the men in robes was, at least at this university, shunned by one and all). But it may have made Robert sorrier he hadn't kept his mouth shut. Why had he chosen to go to the student newspaper? He could no longer quite remember what had prompted his decision. Even though he did his best to put aside everything belonging to the realm of emotions (his respect for academia, his distrust of authority), he was still not sure whether he ought to have defied his supervisor in such a way. Is it right to raise one's voice when being oppressed? Yes. On the other hand, perhaps his supervisor had more to lose. After all, he was nearing the end of his career, not the beginning. And was supplying the journalism students with a story to use as a course assignment really an aid to university policy?

Robert took his pillow and pressed it against his face. He rolled over aggressively, as if turning his back on a woman lying next him; then he threw the pillow onto the floor and stared up at the rafters of his room. Only then did he notice he was crying. Ten minutes later he was asleep.

Chapter V

The air was endowed with a bracing chill that alluded to the winter ahead; chilly enough, in fact, to turn Robert's breath to steam as he descended the Neroberg toward the old city center. He had decided to go to the library for a while before returning home for lunch. It felt good to have a destination, he thought, as he strolled down the boulevard, politely smiling to a lady walking her dog.

"Why," he thought suddenly, "didn't I become a surfer?" A pure, independent way of life, as fresh as the ocean air, appeared before his mind's eye; whoever cannot say "Yes" to society should at least declare the "No" of the drifter. And yet it was impossible to consider this seriously. Nor could he see himself becoming a businessman, though it may very well feel like a never-ending thrill ride, and (although it pained him to admit it) the lifestyle appealed to his tastes. He had not been able to become a rock star or a poet, nor could he have succeeded among those cynics who believe in nothing but money and power. He forgot his age. He imagined he was still twenty, and still had all the hopes and choices of the world before him.

Just then a Polish girl from class walked by without noticing him; impulsively, he tapped her on the shoulder, but rather than greeting him she just stared at him. For a moment they gave each other a measuring look, and, consequently, after a few seconds of silence, it dawned on Robert that this was *not* a Polish girl from Deutschkurs. Of the ten billion synapses in his brain, none of them wanted to spark. He could say *"Hallo, wie geht's"* in German, but he couldn't speak it. Worse yet, this woman was waiting for him to say something. She didn't walk away like a merciful human should. He racked his brains to place her. If she wasn't one of the women from Deutschkurs, then who was she? Could she have been a friend of his host family? Had he seen her walking at the park? He began to stutter, but, just as she was ready to walk off, a lone brave synapse decided to shoot a bit of electricity to its partner: "Café Parsival!"

She smiled and ten billion synapses rejoiced. Of course, it was the woman he had seen last week when he had the headache: the blonde in the awning-chair. "I take it you speak English," she said, attempting to communicate with Robert, who was too stupefied to speak. Hence she began to interrogate him with the sad result of one-syllable answers, and, suffice it to say, it was time for prince charming to take the offensive.

"Uh, you speak English well" he said, followed by a pathetic smile. He almost said, "Your accent is so cute, you must speak German well"—but stopped just in time; and in light of this, his first comment appeared better.

"You know, it's funny," she said, swinging her handbag lightly in her hand, "I noticed you that evening because you looked so foolish. My friends and I were talking about you as we were pretending to look at our photos. We laughed when we thought about the poor lonely man having to deal with five women staring at him."

Robert let out a chuckle and then asked himself what he was doing in the middle of the street getting analyzed by a woman he didn't know. In spite of this, he found a certain pleasure in seeing her up close. She was gorgeous.

"And what do you do for a living, anyway?" he asked.

"I'm an editor for a small press in Mainz."

"Do you like your job?" he asked without any particular inflection; and when she had answered in the affirmative, he jumped at the chance to ask her out for a coffee. Just as quickly, she refused the invitation, explaining that she had been at the *Wiesbadener Kurier* all morning and had to return to Mainz for lunch.

"That's too bad," he sighed.

"No it's not," she said; and then she jotted down her name and number on a piece of paper, handed it to him, smiled and rushed off in the direction in which she had originally been heading. Her number was from Wiesbaden, and when Robert read her name, Monika, he would never think of her again as the Hollywood Star.

Chapter VI

The family was below eating breakfast. When Robert was home, he usually stayed in his room, and it had been some time since he last said hello. He leaned forward over the nightstand and opened the window. The entire room, excluding the A-frame ceiling, was of such dimensions that one could easily reach the window, unlatch it and open it without getting out of bed. A chilly rain had started to drum on the yellow and orange leaves that framed his secluded panorama. This landscape, rather busy and whimsical, though somber in color, looked like a painting as viewed through the window of his room. In the distance one could see church spires poking out from the city, and up the hill, perched on their misty crest, were the golden cupolas of the Russian Chapel, veiled in grayness, losing themselves in the hazy banks that settled in the trees and clung to the vineyard slopes.

Robert stood motionless for what seemed like a very long time. Then, when all had become still, he descended the narrow wooden staircase that connected his attic to the rest of the house, tiptoed across the dining room, and crept into the kitchen. He was by nature stealthy-footed and such conditions brought his feline cautiousness to full expression. "Interesting," he thought. Moments earlier this family had been in this room, interacting with each other as if there were no one else in the house. He started to open cupboards and peek in drawers. He moved appliances, checked the fridge, and even looked in the trash bin. Then he left the kitchen and, advancing again on tiptoe, entered the living room where he began to pull books from shelves, flipping pages with the hope of finding a letter or a note—something that would reveal the hidden life behind this seemingly wholesome family. The dining table was breathtaking; it must have dated to the nineteenth century with an immaculately polished parquet top and carved legs resembling the talons of hawks clutching balls. He grabbed the vase centered on the table and looked beneath it.

Then he saw it. Across the room, behind glass, illuminated by a halogen lamp, was a clock of old Meissen china. This fine porcelain, originating from what is today a suburb of Dresden, has a particular blue tint, often depicts scenes of eighteenth century aristocracy partaking in leisurely activities and is found in most museums of applied arts. Robert approached the cabinet—not without a feeling that he was doing something wrong—and ever so cautiously opened it. The ceramic glistened in the light. He grasped it and held it high in the air so as to make its bottom visible, shaking it and listening for the rattle of a telltale sign, so preoccupied with finding something that he quite forgot the value of this object. It was older than his country, for God's sake! He gave it another shake, this time harder. Something had been placed in a hole near the clock mechanism. Robert stuck his finger in, far enough to touch what felt like a ring. Then he heard a strange sound: a fascinating jingling followed by a crank and then a loud click. It was like a key turning in a door...the front door. The family was back!

The shock created by the realization that he was about to be caught red-handed with his host family's prized possession caused his heart to pump three beats worth of blood in one great contraction. His first impulse was to get the clock back into the case. Naturally, he imagined the family would be curious as to what he was doing in their living room, but his hands were shaking terribly, the clock was slick from his sweaty grip and the latch to the cabinet was jammed. It was so bad he nearly dropped the blasted thing! He was literally paralyzed from panic as a million thoughts surged through his mind, none of them stopping long enough to provide an excuse. "I'm going to faint," flashed across his mind, but the door was taking a while to open, and he at once recovered his balance. He tossed the old clock on the table and, in an inspiring display of courage, made a dash for his room, practically taking flight as he leapt up the narrow staircase four steps at a time.

The family entered happily chatting, unpacking bags, hanging coats, laughing, and then stopped. An uneasy silence followed.

Robert stood frozen in the center of his room, his heart beating so violently that it hurt him. He knew that at that very second they were standing before the dining table, looking in astonishment at the clock haphazardly thrown on it. Noticing the empty shelf and disheveled books, they would put two and two together and figure out that the culprit had just been there, and must still be in the house with them. They would guess that he couldn't have escaped through the front door and the back door was still locked from the inside. "Robert," a voice called—it was the husband—"are you there?" Then, with a quiver in her voice, the wife followed suit. Robert didn't answer. He realized all too painfully the shame of getting caught snooping through these people's affairs; besides, even if he wanted to feign innocence, he had already gone too far to pretend it wasn't him.

Thus, he quietly stepped inside his closet, but before he had a chance to duck behind a jacket, the door to his room flew open and the two owners of this house came in. The husband breathed Robert's name, this time on edge, in a tone so low as to almost be a whisper. There was movement near the bed, the window was opened and closed, and they were talking about him—oh yes, even when we don't understand the language, we know when we're being talked about. Then the closet door began to open with a creak. The two parents turned to see what happened. They paused for a moment, staring at the closet. Then they walked out. He could hear them climbing down the creaky wooden staircase, and then calling the police and describing the clock. He stood motionless in his closet, for at least fifteen minutes, until they left.

Now it may well be that Robert's host family was not calling the police; it's true that they showed no particular concern for their guest, and Robert was allowed all the liberty any visitor could wish for. Be that as it may, after this little fiasco, he sneaked out of the house, descended the hill, and would swear that walking down the Taunusstrasse was a feeling of bliss unequalled since years. "That's one to tell the guys back home," he thought, breathing a deep, joyful sigh with the whole of his lungs. Indeed, now that he was free and able to see the situation in a somewhat better light, he could not for the life of him imagine how they didn't see him in the closet. All that mattered now, thank God, was that they didn't. The weather was crisp, and all the lovely people were out shopping. Robert stopped at a bookstore, still jittery, but calm enough to wave to the clerk as if to say "It's me again," and then he checked the bargain bin— nothing special. He continued along until the bottom of the Taunusstrasse where he stopped at the Kochbrunnen for a drink of hot mineral water.

Translated literally, the word means *Boiling Fountain*: *Koch* (pronounced like "coke" but with a soft and scratchy letter "k") is cognate to the English word *cook*, though in modern German *kochen* means *to boil*. *Brunnen* means *fountain*. To mark the spot, a neoclassical dome stands over the marble basin with oddly shaped spouts from which the malodorous liquid continually flows. The impression made by this curious architecture is not unlike the feeling of trekking through the hustle and bustle of a modern city, surrounded by cold, clean cement, shining metal and mirrored glass, and then stumbling across an ancient ruin. The sight immediately sweeps one away to another time and another place. Gazing at the structure, Robert was suddenly reminded of his girlfriend: that peculiar quality of the past to stick out and taint the present, to declare itself and its beauty against the optimism of the present, and to remind us of our roots. He opened his wallet and looked at her picture. Indeed, it was just as out of place as this dome overhead.

Robert turned around. He was now standing next to an old man wearing a furry overcoat and a Russian winter hat. If this guy was trying to capture the style of a Cossack, he was doing well. Wiesbaden does have some characters running around. God knows where they come from. Robert took a sip. It was uncanny. The water has a particular, salty flavor that once tasted is never forgotten. It is not for the timid of palate and newcomers are easily identified by their contorted facial expressions and fear of swallowing. The man was staring at him. Robert attempted to smile, but received nothing in return, only this insidious gaze that was becoming more gripping by the second. Then, with a wave of his cane, he spoke; but what he said didn't entirely make sense. He whispered the words as if to reveal a secret: "It's hotter than you think."

It was a strange thing to say. Robert wasn't sure whether to interpret it as a sincere, friendly warning ("Please don't burn yourself; I've seen others do it a thousand times") or as irony ("I know what you're thinking and I can see you don't belong here.") It wasn't even sure if it was intended for Robert. But then to whom? The two were standing there alone; and Robert had just drunk a cup right in front of his face. Whatever the message meant, Robert heeded it and emptied the cup back into the fountain. It was as if the headache that had been bothering him last week was returning with the stress of being observed; but before Robert could regain his faculties, the old man was gone.

Chapter VII

The Café Klappe, located on a narrow street near the Parsival, has a bar in the shape of a clapper board (the thing that gets clapped in front of a movie camera at the beginning and ending of a take). The place is decorated with wooden tables, pocked brick walls and movie posters here and there, the most impressive being an original for Fritz Lang's *Metropolis*. There weren't many people, but enough to add a comfortable hum of small talk and the tinkle of someone's spoon in a glass. Even more pleasing was the "shish" of the espresso machine and the strong scent of fresh-ground coffee in the air. Robert, oblivious to the beauty of this scene, gazed into the yellow spirals of foam as the sugar lost itself in the whirlpool he had just created in his cup.

He was thinking about how things and people seemed to go around in disguise. The host family, which had been beaming with smiles on their visit to his home in America, now barely looked at him when he was at home. At first glance, the woman at the Parsival looked like a pretentious fashion nymph, but she was actually quite normal when he spoke to her in the street. And let us not forget: this quiet, well-groomed town held in its historical coffers the vilest of crimes. Where were the scars? Indeed, where were the Germans? Everyone seemed to speak English around here. Everyone appeared to be a part of the same middle class found in the middle class of every other country in the world. The radios played the same hits, the bookstores displayed the same books; and one was much more likely to encounter pizza, hamburgers and Thai curries in their daily diet, than sauerkraut, schnitzel and bockwurst.

Suddenly Robert found himself thinking of that old man he had met at the fountain. What had he said? Something about the water. Robert summoned all his wits to bring back that scene in his mind. The old man warned him about the water; but that's it! He warned him in English! For some reason this revelation struck Robert as monumental in significance. Again and again he returned to that situation: how long had the old man been standing there when he spoke? What was he wearing? And what had been the sequence of events? First Robert drank; then the man spoke. There was something odd about that. Robert had drunk a whole cup before the old man gave the warning. When did the old man arrive? And how did he know Robert spoke English? Granted, clothing can betray one's nationality, even gestures, a sneeze, the clearing of a throat or one's gait; but, still, Robert didn't speak to him, or anyone else in his presence; and isn't that a bit presumptuous to give an order without first asking the recipient's origins? Another flash came: he whispered.

Robert knocked back his espresso in one sip. "Enough is enough!" he thought. He wondered if everyone had such flights of fancy, or was it the result of traveling to a new country and spending too much time alone. Anyway, he didn't want to be alone today, not again; and thus he opened his little black book and looked through the names and numbers—all one of them. The only name from Wiesbaden other than his own was Jürgen's. He found a phone near the restroom, inserted his card and dialed. Suddenly a woman's voice came on the line. He had forgotten Jürgen lived with his girlfriend. Politely, he asked for Jürgen, and after a pause his friend popped on the line ranting about a man who was fined two thousand Euros for jogging naked in Freiburg. Robert breathed a sigh of relief, and then invited him to coffee. It was clear, "obviously and absolutely" clear: this was the perfect way to spend the afternoon, as long as Robert didn't mind his girlfriend coming along.

Jürgen's girlfriend was an intelligent-looking woman with auburn hair, high cheekbones and almond eyes with lashes that seemed to spill over her cheeks. To say she was a head-turner was an understatement; at least three other men were checking her out as she entered the café. She was holding the French version of "The Plague" by Camus, and when she approached Robert, politely taking his quivering hand in hers, she introduced herself in remarkably clean English as Petra.

"That's a nice name," Robert rejoined. "Are you French?"

"As a matter of fact, no," she said, letting go of his hand. "No one in my family is French, none of my friends are French, and I don't think I've ever visited France longer than two weeks."

Although one could detect an accent, she spoke quite brightly, and rather precisely, in a cultivated, if not distant voice. She was one of those chic, European women whose extreme tidiness—everything polished, mended, brushed up and color coordinated—suggested more fastidiousness than wealth. There was something pent-up about her; a look of mistrust, of apprehension, and, in addition, she was thin.

"Are you German?" Robert asked.

"Of course."

In an attempt to avoid another less than brilliant question, Robert turned to greet Jürgen who paused for a moment, and then held his finger in the air like an old man about to scold a child. "Robert," he said with the face of a boy proud for what he had learned, "do you realize that German citizenship comes from the nationality of the parents—the blood in your veins, pal—and not by the place of birth?"

The starter's pistol had been shot and Jürgen was off. He continued on this train of thought, explaining something about Prussians in Wiesbaden and Germans in Russia, the two world wars and the founding of the German Confederation after 1815; speaking loudly enough that at least the next two tables could hear him. For his girlfriend this was apparently all nonsense. She leafed through her book as if his oratory were a radio that had been left on in the kitchen. Then he boldly professed that "America, on the other hand, is defined by land. If you're born on American land, you can have American citizenship." Whereupon Petra crossed her legs, and then uncrossed them, looked up and frowned, ready to veto the whole conversation, but Jürgen didn't give her a chance to speak. Rather, he pushed on and said: "Yes Robert, to be American is to be born there."

"Ultimately," Robert added, fiddling with a sugar cube, "to be American is to live there. There's no such thing as an American language, or an American race. Amerigo Vespucci was a sailor, not a culture. Navajo exists as a culture, race and language, but American does not. The cultures, races and languages of America are continually changing, and yet the borders stay fixed."

Jürgen listened to this remark with casual interest and then paused, dramatically assuming a face of great concentration. He took off his glasses, placed them on the table, and with his shirtsleeve wiped a bead of sweat from his brow. Then his forehead illuminated: "Yes, perfect Käfer's talk! I'm sure he would like it. Why do we always begin these topics in the wrong places? We must meet on a Thursday night."

"But Jürgen" demanded Robert, "What's this place you keep talking about?"

"We call it the regular meeting point," he said, putting his glasses back on and waving for the bill. "I'm sure you'll like it, and I promise I'll invite you soon. I'm sorry, pal, but we must go. Give us a call, okay."

"Wait, wait a minute!" Robert contested, grabbing Jürgen's arm. "And what do you mean, we? Is this some kind of club you're in?"

"He likes to call us the Knights of Pythias," Jürgen replied, as if this were common knowledge. Then, despite his glib manner, he gave Robert a confidential look, and added: "But it's much more than that."

Petra winked. Robert lifted himself out of his chair to take her hand, but they were already out the door, shouting back not to forget the New Year's Eve party and laughing as they disappeared up the street. Suddenly a gust of wind caught the front door and slammed it shut with a loud bang. Everyone in the café jumped. Such wild and volatile weather lately; as if the two were somehow linked, Robert pondered Jürgen's suspicious hint. As a rule this sort of thing didn't interest him. Sometimes, however, the curiosity would strike, like the wind, and he could think of nothing else than the little inconsistencies in his life.

Chapter VIII

"No," Robert answered. "I'm definitely not the type to enjoy public nudity. I mean, I come from a place where bathing suits hang down to your knees. Speedos belong in the Olympics, not on the beach, and prancing around naked in a fountain in Rome is not my idea of fun. Of course I like my body and all. I guess just not that much."

For some reason Jürgen found this funny. He also didn't seem to mind calling at nine in the morning, shocking Robert out of a sound sleep. Hardly had Robert put out the reading lamp the night before when the sleep overcame him. He had slept undisturbed and dreamed intensely—something about running but being unable to move, followed by a frightening view of the back of his own head. Upon hearing Jürgen's voice it vanished. Apparently, he was phoning to thank Robert for the coffee they had shared the day before. He was also keen to have Robert's opinion of his girlfriend, to which Robert couldn't come up with anything beyond a few polite comments at the most general level. "Some of my friends don't like her at all," he explained, "but she seems to think you're okay." Robert expressed all the gratitude a man could give at nine in the morning. Then Jürgen got a call on the other line and the conversation was over.

The thought of spending another day in bed was unbearable; the mere consideration of which caused Robert's heart to flare up in stress. He pushed the covers down to his feet and forced himself to rise. Jürgen's call had left him in a mood to visit someone, and yet there was no one to visit. A walk into town would surely provide some entertainment. After all, the air was fresh, the shops were open, and God knew what people were roaming the streets.

After a stroll along the Taunusstrasse, he had veered off onto a broad sidewalk, the main street, obviously, of an elegant spa. Along one side of the street was a medley of buildings with balconies, verandas and sculpted facades. On the other side was a park. Robert continued along at a brisk pace with both hands stuck in his pockets. All about were ladies young and old, laden with shopping bags, appearing and disappearing into boutiques. Despite the chilly weather, many of them were wearing skirts and even more were sporting v-neck blouses and pumps, which, unfortunately, did not become them all alike. Here and there were handsome show-windows displaying handbags from Paris, boots from Milan, and watches made in Switzerland. This was the beloved Wilhelmsstrasse, as in Kaiser Wilhelm, and one could sense this town was proud of it. This was Wiesbaden's show-window to the world. The annual street party, Jürgen said, was the only festival in Germany where more champagne was consumed than beer.

Ahead was the Kurpark; the lush gardens behind the Kurhaus where Dostoevsky once relaxed after nights of gambling (today a bust commemorates the event). It was a lovely autumn day and the park was speckled with visitors, some taking a late-afternoon constitutional, others enjoying the picturesque surroundings. Robert found a bench that afforded a splendid view of the grounds, the centerpiece of which is a lake with a fountain spraying water into the air. At the next bench a gray-haired gentleman with scarf and hat was sitting legs crossed and reading a newspaper. Two ladies walked by excitedly talking. A young boy, no older than four, attempted to feed some ducks at the lake's edge while his grandmother stood at a safe distance superintending the work with an occasional shout. The air was heavy with the scent of moist earth; and leaves of gold and red gently twirled in the breeze.

Robert opened his wallet and took out the piece of paper on which was written a telephone number and the name Monika. For a long time he stared at the name with its six steadfast characters, triadic syllables and Teutonic letter "k". Then he tightened his scarf around his neck and made off in search of a payphone near the Kurhaus. He found one inside, next to the entrance to Käfer's, and on the second ring she answered by stating her family name: "Wieland." He cleared his throat, greeted her in English and before he could finish explaining his experiment into the philosophical benefits of unemployment, she asked him out for a drink, at a place called the Philharmonie.

It took about twenty minutes to get there by foot. From the street the place has the appearance of an old apothecary, and in many respects the interior equally smacks of the chemist's décor. All around are shelves filled with old books and curios, portraits of composers, various knickknacks, trinkets and whatnot. Robert sidled up to the bar and took to examining some books on the shelf; and, after a while, his date arrived, introducing herself with some kisses on the cheeks. Her bobbed, silky-blond hair looked as though it had been cut that day, brushing her cheeks with every spin of the head. Robert smiled and guided her to a seat with his hand. The two ordered some drinks and Robert sparked the conversation with a question about cultural events in and around Frankfurt. Monika smiled and the two began talking about this and that, museums in Germany, windsurfing and California, American movies and Monika's experience as an au pair in Paris when she was nineteen.

But it wasn't long before she asked him what he did for a living. Robert, meanwhile, had finished his drink and was now attempting to call over the bartender for a refill. She asked him a second time. He nervously cleared his throat and informed Monika (the woman who had smiled to him in the café, given him her phone number, and invited him to this bar) that he was in Europe doing research for his thesis. He was ashamed. He knew that the real reasons behind his decision to come to

Germany would appear irresponsible to someone who worked for a living. He thought to unbosom himself and tell the story of his crisis and of Sybille and how she helped him pack his bags and go. But in the end he did not. From Monika's point of view, Sybille's attempt to help him leave could only appear foolish; and even if Robert were to muster the courage to expose his weaknesses, he was not ready to allow anyone to think ill of his girlfriend.

I think I like you, her gaze seemed to whisper; but she refrained from saying it. "Sounds interesting," she said coolly and Robert jumped on the opportunity to change the subject, asking how long she had been working as an editor.

"Let's see," she thought, scratching her head, "this is my third month now."

"Third month?" Robert laughed.

"After my studies I returned to Paris and found a job with a magazine. Two years ago I returned to Hamburg." Then she paused, pinching her lips in a wistful, almost penitent way. "At first it seemed to be the right choice, but later I realized it was taking me away from what was important."

It's amazing, Robert thought, how a life sounds so interesting when we're hearing it for the first time. "But why Wiesbaden?" he asked.

"I don't know," she admitted. "I joke to myself that I'm here for the water."

"At least you're not here for the nightlife," Robert returned, and at this display of humor, Monika broke out laughing, her face instantly transforming from that of a cultured woman to a bright-eyed girl. Then she asked if Robert had a rich family.

"I'm afraid not," he admitted. If she only knew, he thought, of the debt he had collected during seven years of university, she would make for the door and forget she had ever met him. "I know," he went on, and then lost his train of thought. He had started to stroke his earlobe (a habit spanning back to his childhood), but then stopped. "I know I should go back home, patch up my 'career' and all that, but between you and I, I have a hard time understanding what that word means."

"I believe it's a form of commitment," she said.

He began to shake his head as someone in anguish, pressing the butt of his hand against his brow. "I know," he said gravely. He sipped his drink and noticed his heart was pounding. A memory arose: his family was at the dinner table of his grandmother's apartment in LA, his parents were still together, and his aunt and uncle were due to arrive at any moment. Father had gotten angry for some reason or other and had stormed out of the room; grandmother broke out laughing. She turned to Robert and stroked his hair. "Laugh and the world laughs with you," she said, "Cry and you cry alone."

Robert looked at Monika and smiled: "You know, I've thought, if only I had grown up poor and wanting, I'd be more focused, driven and hungry for success, or at least not take what I have and have achieved for granted."

"Are you saying that you regret not having been poor?"

"I"—he couldn't continue. It was evident that this idea had troubled him before and that she had startled it to life again. She had uttered feelings he was wont to suppress. "I don't know what I'm saying."

"But don't you want anything?"

"You bet I do. I want everything. That's my problem."

She smiled. "I like that about you."

As she spoke, he looked at her and thought how ravishing she was, savoring every motion of her lips, and examining her face. It was difficult to pay attention to the conversation, which was no more than a thinly veiled excuse to be close to her. He wondered if she was experiencing the same, and if her mind was wandering like his, imagining them as a couple, as a family, and how it would be to share his life with her. The unresolved romantic tension could have fuelled the discourse all night long. God, she had lovely hands.

Chapter IX

Sybille had a peculiar way of letting someone know she was angry: she would talk about her legs. Since childhood she had heard comments about her strong limbs, by grade school she was running at track meets and throughout her high school years sports—field hockey and tennis, in particular—played a central role. It was quite clear from photos that she was an attractive young woman with a body that must have garnered much attention; and, considering that Germans have no scruples about prancing around and photographing themselves in the nude (Sybille's logic was: if not when you're young, then when?), the chance for sharing her charms with the world wasn't lost. By the time Robert met her, however, she had become convinced her legs were "thick" (which could have meant "fat" or "thick" depending on how her German mind was translating the German word *dick*), and, for reasons unknown, regardless of the bone which had been picked or the reason for a particular dispute, the subject of her thick legs ended up dominating every fight.

Robert loved her legs. From the very first time he met her while doing fieldwork in Northern California (at Fort Ross in Sonoma County, a Russian Fort dating to 1830; she was visiting the site while on holiday), a secret voice in him begged to get to know those legs better. And yet is it likely that her legs sparked a three-and-a-half year relationship? Probably not; the secret voice in question was surely that of Sybille herself; and, after years of sharing her unusual self-perception—or rather self-consciousness—Robert found her legs growing ever more significant in his thoughts. Suffice it to say, the memory is a funny thing, and there are pessimists who believe the past will forever slip through our fingers. But please don't worry: as the subject now touched upon has been dealt with in many clever and well-informed books, neither here nor later will any serious attempt be made to offer a meditation on the subject of memory, and thus enter into competition with philosophy.

Churning such thoughts over and again, Robert made his way through the streets of the old city center: the Goldgasse with its cafés and restaurants, the Mühlgasse with its florist, clothing boutiques and delicatessen; and on the Römertor where the remains of a Roman wall are found. He was fond of walking these streets late in the afternoon, when the sky began to darken and the rush of shoppers brought out the greatest variety of faces—but today his head was aching; and the further the afternoon wore on and the thicker twilight became, the more his impressions, too, became confused and burdensome. He headed up one of the streets in need of a place to sit down. There was a bench in the Kurpark that would suit this purpose; and if he was going to the Kurpark, then why not to the Kochbrunnen for a dose of the liquid that seemed to intensify his moods? As he thought and walked, his destination was nearing. He arrived with a thirst.

The scene was calm today. There were no children playing in the square, no bums on the lawn, and no retirees filling bottles from the fountain. Robert approached the source alone, and the moment he passed beneath the arch, he felt a distinct change in mood. He couldn't put his finger on it, but there was something enticing about this place. Maybe it was the flowing water, and that it had continued uninterrupted for millennia, that it was older than history, and thus beyond it. Or Nature: that it had survived thousands of years of Culture and would surely outlast it. For drinking from this spring felt like tapping the earth itself, toasting a sacred union with the unfathomable depths from which this fluid rises, plumbing Hadean chasms where soil, water and mineral unite in a molten soup.

Robert took his glass from his backpack and with a ritual attention rinsed it three times before filling it. The burning libation bubbled and swirled in its goblet, as if reluctant to be taken. He took a sip, paused for a moment, letting the bitter draft rest in his mouth, and then swallowed in a single, pyretic gulp. He quickly filled another glass, guzzled it down and focused on the warmth that stoked this waxing delirium, inhaling the sulphurous fumes that stung the nostrils and deadened the senses. There was something in the air, an oddly spectral presence whispering in the vapors, lulling him into a peculiar repose.

He filled his lungs and held it as long as he could. Then it hit him: His head began to reel. It felt as if he were drunk, as though he had been struck with a fever, drawing blood from his cheeks, seizing his breath; something in the lower back, weakening his limbs. Be it of drug or germ, he was caught in the throes of a bewildering force, as if he were on a ship rolling in heavy seas, as if the ground itself were pitching and swelling, causing his hands to desperately reach out for something firm. The pulsating ache was relentless, raging in his head like a tempest. He closed his eyes and pressed his temples; and when he opened them again, he had a queer feeling. He felt a woman was there with him.

Chapter X

It was getting on towards dark when Robert arrived back at his room, which meant he had been walking all day. What paths he had taken through the forest and what streets he had taken through the city were already a faded memory. All he knew was that he had covered most of the city center, two parks and the length of the pedestrian zone; and he had still managed to accomplish nothing. He couldn't even remember what he had thought about. Only a displeasing sensation of restlessness remained. His address book caught his eye. On the one hand, he had been seeing a lot of Jürgen. On the other hand, there was no one else to call. He picked up the phone, dialed, and then before he could finish saying his name, Petra's voice was on the line.

"I'm so happy you called!" she exclaimed. "Jürgen is out for the evening—Thursday night, you know—his silly meeting at Käfer's, The Knights of the Babbling Madman, or whatever they call themselves, but I'm free and if you wish, you can stop by for a drink and a chat. I'm still reading this book and the descriptions are repulsing me. I can't bear the thought of spending the evening with it. Please come over and distract me. I'm begging you. I demand it!"

Jürgen and Petra's apartment was in the Westend, some fifteen minutes from the Neroberg. As soon as Robert arrived (via bus line number one, past the main station and along the Kaiser Friedrich street direction Ringkirche), he was won over with the neighborhood. Whereas the Neroberg was dotted with villas, parks and vineyards, the Westend was a continuous sprawl of urban dwellings, giving one the pleasant misimpression of being in a big city. Robert found his destination and rang Petra from the street below. She greeted him through a crackly speaker, instructing him to take the stairs to the top floor (there was no elevator) and opened the door with a loud buzz.

The moment one entered the apartment, one was confronted with an overwhelming mural of Max Weber; so big you could count the hairs on his beard. Weber, looking like a cross between a pharmacist and a bulldog, was the influential sociologist who taught around the turn of the century at the universities of Freiburg, Heidelberg and Munich. Robert had heard of him at Berkeley, but never dreamt of reaching this level of appreciation for the man.

The rest of the flat was equally interesting. Books were everywhere—everywhere but the bookcase. The bed was unmade and consisted of nothing more than a mattress on the floor. Next to it was a brand new stereo system with speakers mounted to the ceiling and next to that a space-aged metal rack with CDs. Since there was only one chair in the room, Petra sat down Indian style on the bed and allowed Robert to sit erect. This arrangement forced him to look down to her when speaking, which he personally objected to. He propped his arm on a long writing desk and smiled apologetically. She noticed his discomfort and said: "We don't buy much, but when we do, it must be the best."

"I like your mural," he returned, inspecting Weber's forehead. This place could use a maid, he thought, noticing a sock stuffed under a pillow. And whatever it was that brought this couple together, Robert would never know. Within moments he could sense that she was the antithesis of Jürgen.

"Oh, without Max, Jürgen and I could never stay together."

"He must have been quite a sociologist."

She began pulling books from the shelf. "He's the only author we both read, not to mention the climax of our New Year's Eve party. Would you like something to drink?"

"Sure. I'll have whatever you're having."

"Fine, do you take your martinis with gin or vodka?"

"With olives, thanks."

Petra, looking pleased, reached behind the books, pulled out a shaker, olives, extra dry vermouth and vodka, and then began to mix a couple martinis. She tasted every ingredient with gusto, not to say fervor; and repeatedly, though with careful avoidance

of flattering language, expressed her satisfaction at having someone with whom she could have some rational conversation.

Robert, looking panicked, tried to live up to her image of
him: "Well," he said observing her pour the vodka. "Well, Petra,
uh—Jürgen sure is an interesting guy—what I mean to say is—
well, what's this club he's in?"

"Please don't ask," she said, violently shaking the drinks.
"I'm actually quite ashamed of it. If you want to know the truth,
it's more of a sect than a club—spooky stuff, hocus-pocus.
Jürgen and a few of his 'nameless' colleagues, as he puts it—you
know, this is part of the mystique—like to meet with a crazy old
man who purports to be the last living alchemist in Europe."

"The last living what?"

"Alchemist. You know, like Merlin the magician, lives in a
dungeon somewhere deep beneath the earth, cooking up potions
and trying to make gold."

"You don't think that's true, do you?" Robert chuckled,
unconsciously slurping his drink. It was just his luck that as soon
as he grasped the subject matter, and thus relaxed, he offended
his hostess by chuckling.

"Of course not," she snapped. "That's the danger in it all. I
know how much fun Jürgen gets out of it, but there's a level
where it's dangerous. It's simply not reality-based, and I don't
trust that double-dealing pied piper that fills his head with so
much rubbish." A vein began to bulge along her left temple
running toward her forehead, like a shadow floating across the
Mona Lisa.

Robert, though stunned by the outburst, found this anger becoming to her. "But—that's really funny—I mean Jürgen seems like such a normal guy."

"And he is. Jürgen is harmless enough. I just worry that he could be too easily swayed by a few fancy words."

"But you don't really think he's the type to join a sect?"

"I don't know," she grumbled. "Once a delusion has you in its grips… Look at the people who gulp down cyanide and strap plastic bags to their heads believing aliens will pick them up in the next world. It seems that twice a day the news reports a case of some nut duping himself into the belief that suicide doesn't kill. Really, if no one believed their misty soul was going to float up to a better life in the clouds, free from the problems we face here on earth, we'd have a lot fewer people dying by their own hand. It sounds amazing, but people are gullible—and they'll do anything to escape the work of survival."

"Maybe you're right," Robert admitted, trying to assimilate this anger, "but I still think people are more rational than you give them credit for."

Petra set her drink on the bookshelf. "Are they?" she asked flatly, and then paused. "I'm pleased to know you're an optimist, but rationalism is a choice, not a drive. And what's so crazy about delusions is that they exist for everyone except the deluded! Once one is detected it's destroyed. Why else do fanatics isolate themselves apart from the subconscious fear of losing their false beliefs?"

Robert laughed. "But you're not going to tell me that people don't have a desire for truth, are you? You make it sound like human nature is defined by lies."

Her brown eyes fixed on him: "How many people are truly conscious of the blood, bone and tissue beneath their skin? Most of us identify with our names, not our organs. We think we're gods or angels or devils, anything but oozing fatty organisms willing to murder for a meal, competing for shelter, trying to get the three-minute chance to reproduce before we wither away and die. Believe me, the last thing people want to know is the truth."

Already by this point in the evening events were getting cloudy. Nevertheless this much was sure: the two ended up in a conversation about philosophy, which bore no fruit other than the discovery that Petra, with her intimidating language skills, had studied the subject in London and Robert was an existential solipsist suffering from self-denial. Then, as one song changed to the next, Robert's hostess placed the third martini in his hand and toasted him with a cheerful "*cin cin*." This one tasted even smoother than the last indicating that as the night progressed, her bartending skills were getting better. Robert decided to change the subject, leaping headfirst into a convoluted argument suggesting there was no connection between art history and the fine arts.

"Not even in the names?" she responded, examining the moisture on her glass.

"The art historian studies artifacts, not aesthetics,"

proclaimed the university dropout who still read comics. "I mean, I find it silly when someone visits a museum and comments on the colors of a painting. A painting is put in a museum because of its historical significance, not its aesthetic value. It's not sold for 45 million bucks because it's pretty!"

"Isn't it?" she countered, licking the rim of her glass rather expressively.

Robert didn't notice, as his over-laden mind attempted to make sense of the jabber coming from his mouth. "Look," he contested, pleading, as if Petra were bombarding him with highbrow theory, "you can't call a Rothko beautiful, if you've seen a Vermeer."

"I like Rothko."

This was the right hook that slipped by, and Robert's argument fell down for the count: "So you like abstraction, do you?"

"But Rothko isn't abstract," she rebutted with a startling flash of sobriety, "he said it himself. He was simply trying to free portrait painting from the human form. His paintings depart from natural representation only to intensify the expression of the subject implied in the title, not to dilute or efface it. I would argue that his canvases of subtle and abundant tones, varying shapes and textures, were as realistic a representation of humanity as that of the old masters. Both are bound to the same medium, and both are attempting to reflect the same essence."

Just as Robert's lips curled to produce a response, he noticed that Petra was dressed quite seductively this evening. Better late than never, but now the black silk beneath her form-fitting skirt filled Robert's mind with every thought save a decent one. As he grasped for words to keep the chat alive, he found himself tilting his head to get a better view. Sure enough, one could see the side of her small and pointy breast through her sleeve. She tilted along with him, not knowing why. He stuttered for a moment, cleared his throat and then tried to spare himself from utter humiliation: "Um...ahem...interestingly, as I was saying—what was I saying?"

"I still think it's pretty," she returned.

"Baby, it's beautiful—I mean, what's pretty?"

"Modern art, silly!"

The two were now completely relaxed. In fact, Petra was so relaxed she forgot to put the vermouth in the fourth batch of martinis. She compensated by serving it with three olives. Then she handed Robert his drink, spilling half of it on his pants, and said "banzai" (she meant to say "*campai*"). She giggled, but Robert didn't respond. Earlier he had been talkative, sprite, as far as his nature permitted, and generally attentive. Now, however, his condition resembled some trance-like state, and at the same time it was as if all the vodka he had drunk, instantly and with redoubled strength, had rushed back up to his head.

"Tell me the truth," Petra asked, changing her tone, "how long are you planning on staying in Wiesbaden?"

Robert winced and then lapsed again into silence. "I don't

know," he admitted at length. "I don't know anything anymore."

"Do you really expect to find a life here in Germany?"

"Are you suggesting I had one to begin with?"

"Yes," she said, setting her glass on the nightstand. "It's no use being optimistic."

She looked him in the eyes, uncrossed her legs and let her body recline into the pillows.

"Petra, if you want the truth, sometimes I feel scared, scared to wake up the next day and find out how empty my life is, that I'm on the wrong track, that the person who I am is not the same as what I really am. I keep asking myself how I can stop being one person and become another. I feel that life is slipping through my fingers—that everything is going the wrong way. I have no idea where it's taking me and I suspect my decision to come here was just another mistake. Do you want to know the truth? I can't see any meaning to my life."

She gently took him in her arms. "Don't you know? That's because life has no meaning. It's difficult growing up and learning this. Many people don't realize it until they're forty, even fifty years old. Some never find out at all."

Robert stayed within her embrace longer than he should have—much longer. In fact, it was such a nice feeling that, unconscious of what was happening, he let himself envelop her, and the two fell into bed. The covers, on their own with no help at all, wrapped themselves around them. Her skirt had slid up above her stomach.

She stroked his ear with her fingers as she continued in her earnest, yet nurturing voice: "It's juvenile to believe one's life is any more meaningful than the next. If you died tomorrow, do you think your lover wouldn't find another mate? Do you think she'd never laugh again, or moan from the pleasure of a touch? Learn to expect nothing from life, because it doesn't owe you anything. And remember, we survive as a group, not as individuals."

His pants had become unzipped bringing her bare stomach against his, guiding her legs between his. Their lips—especially hers, her full, pouting lips—were almost touching, so close he could feel her breath. They paused for a moment looking at each other. Robert let his lips slowly come toward hers, as his thoughts melted into a blur.

Chapter XI

Robert woke up with a splitting headache and the ringing of the telephone in his ear. It was Monika, fresh and alert as a woman who hadn't saturated her body with intoxicants the night before, calling to see if her Romeo was interested in a date. For a moment, she thought she had dialed the wrong number, as Romeo's voice resembled something from a horror movie. As luck would have it, though, she was planning a "special evening" next Friday at the Philharmonie; and for a moment his voice perked up, long enough to guarantee punctuality.

Hardly had the receiver dropped when he became aware of his headache again, and, along with this awareness, came the painful awareness of his contribution to the Vodka industry. With all of his force he attempted to lift himself up, but only got as far as the foot of his bed. His back was hunched and his head hung down like a dead weight. Then, placing his elbows on his knees, he pressed the palms of his hands against his temples. His entire body was aching; his head was spinning, his feet were numb, and his kidneys felt like someone had beaten them with a bat.

By three, it was time to break some bread and take a walk. He was still exhausted; but he was at least on his feet and ready to perform his ritual of washing up in which a basin in the corner of his room, a disposable razor and some soap played the principal parts. He buried his face in a steaming cloth, rinsed his mouth with the tap water and made sure to give himself a good close shave. He grimaced to himself in the mirror, his cheeks white with lather, and raised his eyebrows up and down at which point he puckered up and blew himself a kiss. He plunged his razor into the sink and violently shook it clean. Then, tugging on the skin below his sideburns, he made a perfect trim.

PART TWO

Albedo

Chapter XII

There is no need to go into detail about the content of Robert's German course: most classes plodded along describing one grammatical aspect or another, and in the end it was difficult to tell one week's lesson from the next. Every so often, though, Robert had the chance to prove his skills, and on this evening the scenario unfolded thus: The teacher began with the word "*groß*" or "big." He then asked a Polish woman behind Robert to give its comparative form. She confidently exclaimed "*größer*," making sure to pronounce the umlaut over the letter "o." The teacher nodded and then asked Robert if he could give the class its superlative form. He sucked in his breath, and loudly proclaimed "*la plus größten*" to which everyone broke out laughing. His error wasn't particularly funny (indeed, it has been said that if you don't know how to pronounce a word, say it loud), but one must experience the tedium of a language class to understand the humor that develops in it. Any excuse to break the tension is immediately leapt upon.

When class ended, one of the Hungarians patted Robert on the back, still chuckling. This was that moment when the classmates, once again, found themselves in the position to interact, not as classmates, but as normal human beings; and yet they still couldn't speak like normal human beings. Robert was putting his books away when the Bosnian greeted him, in English, her command of it coming as a surprise.

Then she gave Robert a strange look: "If you don't mind my asking," she said, "what are you doing here? I thought everyone wanted to live in America?"

"That's true," Robert returned; "everyone except the Americans."

She continued to look at him strangely: "Are you a student?"

"Well, not really. I'm here to learn the language."

"The language?" she repeated. "But, why German? Do you really think you need it?"

Robert wavered. "It is one of the biggest languages in the world, if you haven't noticed."

"Yes, of course. But why do *you* want to learn it?"

"Me?" he asked, caught off guard by the simplicity of the question. "I, I don't know...I like to learn, I guess."

She smiled and heaved a deep sigh. "Well, that's as good an answer as any. And anyway, if you have time you should do your best to enjoy it. If I've learned anything about immigration, the free time at the beginning doesn't last long."

"Uh, that may be," stuttered Robert, "but I'm not an immigrant. I'm just visiting."

She laughed heartily. "Trust me, friend, we all are."

"Immigrants?"

"Visiting!"

Robert couldn't help but laugh too, and jumped on the opportunity to invite her for a coffee. "Well," she said, "you see my husband and children are waiting for me at home, and if I don't visit them at least once in a while, I'll forget their faces. But you're obviously free, or you wouldn't have invited me. Why don't you come over?"

It didn't take long to reach Nermina's place via bus line eight toward a suburb just south of the city. Her apartment was cramped and cluttered, humbly decorated, and yet inviting to the visitor. The living space consisted of a room with a linoleum area in the corner serving as the kitchen. There was a couch, two beds and an overloaded bookcase with a television squeezed in among the volumes and periodicals. On one wall was a poster of Belgrade and, near the corner, a map of the world. Beneath the map was a desk and computer. In front of the computer was Nermina's husband.

"Hello!" hollered the robust, 40-something year old man, waving from behind without losing his bond to the screen: "Radovan. Make yourself at home."

Their two children—a boy aged four and a girl aged three; both with black curly hair—introduced themselves and attempted to greet him in English.

"So you're Nermina's latest victim," continued the burly man, busily ticking and tapping on his keyboard. "Did she tell you you were looking too thin, or did she invite you over 'to visit'? She's tired of me. I know her cooking."

"I must admit," Robert added, "I was born hungry."

"Stay around here and you won't die that way," the man said accompanied by a guffaw; and then he slapped his knee and mumbled to himself, although it was difficult to tell if he was reacting to Robert's joke or something on his computer: "A few more words here and—sit back, enjoy yourself. Yes, that's it!"

While Robert waited for his food, the children went into the bedroom, undressed and bathed themselves without help in the water that Radovan had drawn for them. Robert expressed wonderment at such independence at ages three and four. Nermina shrugged and handed him a bowl of soup. Radovan, meanwhile, continued to gaze into his screen, mouse in hand, going on about the atrocious state of global politics; then he asked if Robert was really American.

"No, I'm not. I'm from LA," Robert said, and then he explained his theory that Californians didn't exist. According to Robert, the whole state was dreamt up by a few misguided pioneers who didn't realize there were indigenous peoples already living there. The idea that there was gold to be found was a lie invented to keep people coming and boost property value. When that stopped working they invented Hollywood.

The food was excellent: cabbage rolls stuffed with juicy ground beef and tomato filling, accompanied by a healthy serving of croquettes. There was also what Nermina called a "winter salad" consisting of pickled cabbage and bell pepper filled with shredded cabbage. But Robert's favorite was called *Sirnitsa*: a cheese tart that melted in the mouth releasing a harmonious burst of herbs, onion, pastry and butter.

"So, my friend," Radovan said, swinging around in his seat, "what did you study in California? Sun bathing?"

Robert stopped chewing. "Actually, I was studying in Canada, but that doesn't matter. I was studying archaeology."

Radovan lit up with excitement. "Now there's a subject!" he cried, breaking away from his computer and running over to Robert. "So it's bones and stones you like! Ah, you knew how to pick a job. Just hearing the word makes me want to grab my bags and head for the field! My buddy from school took it up and now he's in Syria, digging at the residence of Alexander the Great, living it up like a real adventurer—the bum! But if you don't mind my asking, what are you doing here in Germany? Are you working on any excavations? The museum in Mainz is quite good. What did you think of it?"

A palpable uneasiness settled on Robert's face. "Well," he said, "to be honest, I haven't been there yet." His hosts became silent. "Actually, I'm in sort of a break at the moment. I just came to Germany to visit some friends of the family."

"What do you mean, 'in a break'?" Radovan said. "You look a bit young to be on sabbatical. As far as I know academia, you should be out meeting peers and writing papers."

"Well, you see, I'm on a sort of vacation. Of course, I'm still working on my thesis. When I have something for my supervisor in spring everything will be fine." Robert's voice fluctuated, breaking into a cough and then a stutter, but before he could get something out, Nermina cut in.

"I didn't know you were still writing."

"Yes, I am." A second pause ensued, this one even longer than the first. Robert's voice was shaking: "I'm not doing much lately, but I'm sure my productivity will come back soon."

Then Radovan cut in. "That's good, because you should never leave your studies behind. Deadlines and supervisors may be bad, but, believe me, being stuck in limbo is worse. That's why I believe that hard work and a fixed goal are the only way to happiness in this world. God knows, I've seen more than a few blokes collapse under the pressure. But forgive me, I'm talking too much. We've only just met and you seem like a rational man."

Robert didn't answer.

Radovan, who had begun delivering this advice partly in order to show friendliness and partly to appease his wife, was naturally somewhat perplexed when, upon concluding his remarks, he glanced at Robert and observed an expression of utter dejection. "Ah, I knew it," he laughed forcedly, patting him on the back. "You're in a nostalgic mood today. All this talk about your beloved rocks and bones has made you long for the field." If he had looked more closely he would have seen that here no nostalgic mood but something quite the opposite was at hand. Nermina had noticed this. She was keeping a fixed and uneasy gaze trained on Robert.

"Yea, I guess you're right," he said, coming out of his daze.

"Anyway," Nermina broke in once more, in a hurry to respond before her husband, "what matters is that we're here together, right. If it wasn't for you taking this 'vacation' as you put it, I wouldn't have met you in Deutschkurs, and we wouldn't be here feeding you. So eat, why don't you!" Having said this, she suddenly, without another word, took Robert's hand and squeezed it.

Robert let go of her hand and put the rest of the Sirnitsa into his mouth, chewing it nervously. He hadn't noticed that he was sweating profusely; dabbing the corners of his mouth with a napkin brought this to his attention and gave him the opportunity to wipe his brow.

Groping for small talk, Nermina explained that she was from Banja Luka. Before she, Radovan and the kids came to Germany they had been living in Sarajevo. All Robert could come up with to show a polite interest was a lame comment about the origins of World War I and the winter Olympics, followed by an even weaker ode to the beauty of Germany.

"Yes, it is," Radovan returned, assuming a serious tone. "But it's difficult here. I get angry when I think that Nermina is working as a cleaning lady. She has a degree in history, for God's sake. She was a successful teacher at home. She's like, 'think of it as a vacation,' but this isn't my idea of a vacation. I don't think I'll be able to learn this language well, and I'm not sure I'll ever understand these people. I mean, they look like people and they talk like people, but I get the feeling there's some invisible barrier between me and them. I wish they'd just lighten up and try being nice. And the strangest thing is that every time I bring the subject up with Germans, they pat me on the back and agree with me! I swear to God, every single one of them is a paradox. For the moment I'm working, but if I ever try to go somewhere else, if I get laid off…And who knows how long this country will keep us. I admit it, I'm scared."

It was already past midnight, and the apologies came pouring from Robert as the realization hit him that he had not only gabbed these people's evening away, but he had eaten all their food. Nermina laughed: the day a guest leaves too early was what she worried about. For her it was normal to have friends stop by anytime—in truth, this was missed from home—and the last thing anyone needed was an invitation.

Chapter XIII

Robert woke from a deep and cleansing sleep to the sound of his telephone. In fact, he was in the midst of an intense dream when the ringing echoed out from the distant reaches of his unconscious, and, no sooner had the noise seized his attention, than the scene vanished leaving him no recollection of where he had just been. His first impression was that it was Monika, but it wasn't her voice on the line. It was Jürgen, chipper as a squirrel, prating away in utter disregard for his friend's drowsiness. He had managed to con Petra into skipping work to take part in what he called his "plan."

"Your plan?" Robert asked.

"Yes!" Jürgen cheered, as if the circus had come to town, "we're going to the Kaiser Friedrich Bad!"

"The what?" Robert asked, yawning.

"You've obviously not been to one of Wiesbaden's bathhouses."

"I don't think I've ever been to a bathhouse," Robert admitted, lifting himself up from the bed and pulling a sock over his foot.

"Good, it will be more a pleasure to be your guide, then."

"Do I need one?"

The bathhouse was tucked among the buildings of the pedestrian zone. It was easily identified, however, by a garden in front with a notice stating that the grounds were for clients only. A few stone steps and two columns stood before the entrance. Robert stopped here and, as he waited for his friends, read an English brochure about the bathhouse. It was quite informative explaining that Wiesbaden had developed around no less than 26 natural springs. In 40 AD, the Romans built a fortification near these springs and named it *Aquis Mattiacis* or "springs of the Mattiaci", a sub-tribe of the ancient *Chatti*. A town developed around the fort and became renowned, as far away as Rome itself, for the curative powers of its natural springs. In 829 AD, "*Wisibada*" appeared for the first time in the records, and, by the 13th century, "Wiesbaden" had advanced to become a royal court and an imperial town. By the 17th century, it was famous as a "spa," and the number of guests seeking rest and recuperation in its 16 bathhouses outnumbered the inhabitants. In 1806, it became capital of the principality of Nassau-Usingen and experienced its first heyday, attracting visitors such as Goethe and Dostoevsky. In 1866, it was occupied by the Prussians and the foundations for a major city were laid under the patronage of Kaiser Wilhelm II. Between 1880 and 1905, Wiesbaden's population doubled (from 52,238 to about 100,000) and the characteristic style of the houses and villas influenced by *Romantic Classicism* and *Art Nouveau* developed to shape the cityscape one sees today.

The Kaiser Friedrich bath, in which the Roman-Irish steam bath is located, was built in 1913 and is the city's center of Balneotherapy, where all sorts of medicinal baths can be taken. The natural hot springs below it, which flow at a constant temperature of 66.4°C, were originally discovered during the second century AD and are used not only for the mineral baths but to heat the building, as well. Of particular interest was a final note at the end explaining that "The temperature of the baths is pleasant for the human constitution, and it does not cause any disturbances to the respiration system or to the circulation."

"What a vocabulary!" he thought. Only in a spa can one see words like that. As far as Robert was concerned, terms like "Balneotherapy" didn't belong in public. And there was something surreal about the history of this place with its references to ancient tribes, curative powers and human constitution. Historical events seemed to blur in the murky depths of time and legend resurfaced in factual form. The brochure recounted the information in a cool, objective prose, and yet there was something unbelievable at its core. Robert had to laugh at it, which was precisely the moment when his friends came sauntering up the street. They warmly greeted him, poking fun at the newcomer, checking if "Plato remembered to bring his toga," and the like. Robert, mocking their self-confidence, assured his two hosts that he was fully prepared for their little pool party.

"And did Plato remember to leave his bathing suit at home," added Petra, to which Robert let out an audible gulp. "But darling," she said, smiling, "of course you know that no clothes are allowed in the bathhouse."

"But, of—no what?" stuttered Robert, realizing at last that he ought to have stayed in bed. Taking advantage of the shock, Jürgen broke in: "You know," he said, winking, "Petra had a good time with you last week. You are such a devil. I can never leave her alone with my friends."

"Don't listen to him," she interrupted, putting her hand on Robert's shoulder. "He's sillier than you are."

The foyer was paved in mosaic and accented with richly carved oak banisters. There were leather seats and brass coat racks, reminiscent of a grand hotel; not a speck was out of place, nor a detail left unattended to. At the far end of the room was a booth where a receptionist, dressed in white like a nurse, waited to take the money needed to pass to the cloak room. Here, behind a counter, another woman—this one wearing a white hat and gloves—distributed towels and soap. At the far end of the room was yet another door. Once inside, the final stop before entering the bathhouse was an antechamber where one deposited one's shoes before continuing to the locker room to change. Simply entering the baths felt as if one were preparing for a Victorian space voyage.

The three travelers met in the locker room and Jürgen began explaining their journey. He emphasized, in so many words, the importance of varying between the hot and cold environments, the affect of humidity on the pores and the psychological ramifications of being submerged. Petra hastened to add that the body yearned to be pure and that corporal stimulation could incite spiritual liberation. Robert, politely smiling and agreeing with everything his hosts had to say, pulled his towel from his backpack being careful not to take his bathing suit along with it.

The three began disrobing. Living in France had accustomed Robert to being around women in monokinis, although he was never the one naked—not to mention the last time he saw his best friend's girlfriend, namely the woman stripping before him, he had managed to "fall" into bed with her, half-spiffed and completely foolish, attempting to share intimate moments. Petra peeled off her pants, pausing for a deviously long moment, and then, glancing at Robert, slowly slid down her underwear. Her skin was fair and her...Robert cleared his throat and looked away. Jürgen proudly stripped and stood to attention, as if someone were to hold up a judge's card and slap a blue ribbon on his naked body. And then Robert followed suit, coyly turning toward his locker, wishing he could enter it.

The fact that Jürgen wasn't circumcised, and Robert was, did not help Robert's composure in this situation. Nevertheless this little difference was interesting. When Robert was born, there was no ritual around the removal of his prepuce. His parents told him it was done in the hospital before he ever made it home. For Jews and Muslims, the event holds great importance. Tahitians must wait until puberty; and then, with the aid of a few close relatives, a sliver of bamboo and a razor blade, they ritually enter adulthood. Robert grew up being told it had been done to him because it was "cleaner"—whatever that's supposed to mean. Humans have survived most of their history without it, and there are billions of healthy people who never did it. At least somebody could have shaken his hand or given him a pat on the back.

"What are you thinking about?" Petra asked. Robert paused but kept his eyes on the floor; his hand was unconsciously reaching for a towel. Then she poked him in the rear and began to giggle. She looked at him as if to say "haven't you seen a naked woman before?" She asked him again what was on his mind. "Oh nothing," he said, looking up and then staring at her as if he had never seen a naked woman before. "I mean nothing big—uh, nothing much. By the way, just how cold is the water in the cold bath?"

As Robert's thin skin hit the icy-cold water, he wished he could have his prepuce back. Jürgen let out a cry of triumph. Petra gradually brought her pale body into the icy pool, like a virgin yielding to a sacrifice, savoring every dropping degree. Jürgen, still wearing his glasses, told Robert to wait at least five minutes before entering the hot bath: this meant until hypothermia set in.

For those who have never had the opportunity to experience an old European bathhouse, the room in which the three were now bathing did not in any way resemble a public swimming pool; rather the elaborate tile work, massive columns lining the pool and the mosaic high overhead lent the atmosphere of an ancient Roman temple. At one end of the pool was a fountain in the shape of a large seashell spilling fresh water. Jürgen approached it, letting its icy libation splash down onto his head. Robert followed suit. Also in the pool were other bathers, mostly older patrons, many of who were quite robust. Whereas the beach suits the sculpted body, the bathhouse curiously inspires corpulence.

Just as Robert's metabolism was coming to a halt, Jürgen

signaled to enter the hot bath. This was a smaller pool attached to the larger in the manner of a Jacuzzi and swimming pool. The three entered, making space in the crowd of fellow bathers. Once again, Jürgen and Petra let out moans of pleasure as Robert made a kind of squeaking noise indicating he had just received a third degree burn.

"Do you get the chance to exercise everyday?" Petra asked, looking into the water.

Robert shifted his body, "I try the best I can," he said, struggling to keep eye contact "I find it helps me think."

"And equally important," Jürgen added, "to achieve clear thought is to overcome physical desire." His glasses had fogged up in the vapors, though it didn't seem to bother him. Then he went on to explain that he would never forget his first experience with an older woman. He was twenty-two and she was forty. She spoke of the Indian Saddhu and of sensual negation. She taught him how to make love without giving up his energy. It was a highly valuable experience (how could it not be?). After a three-and-a-half-month affair, they finally achieved union and then swore to never speak again; she shook young Jürgen's hand, took a lock of his hair and that was that.

Petra, meanwhile, had let her thigh ever so gently press against Robert. At first, the move went unnoticed as Robert was making a sincere attempt at following Jürgen's train of thought; some time around the comment on the Saddhu, however, Robert distinctly sensed the slow rubbing against his thigh, accompanied by a gentle stroke of her hand. The feeling of this wandering hand softly caressing his flesh, now and then pulling on his leg hairs, amidst the warm bubbling currents was unbearably stimulating and Robert, completely against his will, found himself becoming aroused. His resources abandoned him as he became solely focused on the fingers coming ever closer to his most sensitive places, while every last fiber of his consciousness, as if in response to an impassioned battle cry, rushed to the lower regions of his body. Indeed, with each millimeter that the touches drew nearer he was overcome with a desire for more, and panic at the effect. Only at length did he notice that the conversation had stopped and Jürgen was staring at him awaiting a response.

"Oh, I love a good story," he said nervously, and then coughed.

Jürgen didn't reply; rather he changed the subject. "Marriage," he declared, "is a hindrance to intimacy." Naturally, by this he meant "real, living marriage," not a piece of paper to suggest one couple is more righteous than the next; and the only way for a couple to keep a relationship alive was to put it to the test at all times and under all conditions. "A relationship is a paradox," he explained. "It only exists as a negative of the reality it projects. If one is not willing to put a few chips on the table, there is no game; and if a man is not willing to allow his partner the freedom to seek out living experience, there is no relationship."

This also required explaining: by "living experience" he meant the sins, affairs and adventures that give us stories to tell when we're old. He believed that regrets were like diseases, and living experience was the only cure. Petra smiled. Robert was ill at ease. "The moment two partners trust each other," he continued, "they have lost each other." For Jürgen, the problem with marriage was that it masked the ever-present risk of infidelity. Of course, a flimsy certificate was no assurance against the sweet temptations of life. It was, however, apt to ease the tension—this all-important, life-giving tension. In his opinion, there was no better remedy for a waning marriage than soft music, low lighting and another man.

It was at this point that Robert began to show his nervousness. Petra splashed him with some water. "Marriage is a nuisance," Jürgen reiterated. It got in the way of testing the relationship; and in the final analysis, it was old-fashioned. "Modern couples," he said, looking at his girlfriend and winking, "don't need it." Then he confessed that he actually got down on his knee one night and asked Petra not to marry him. She nodded her agreement. This was possibly the closest they ever got to romance.

The threesome jumped into the cold bath (more precisely: the twosome jumped into the cold bath and one waited a few minutes before climbing out of the Jacuzzi) and after a while returned to the hot bath (with a different seating arrangement). But this time nothing was said; all that filled the mind were the vapors. It was difficult to judge how much time had passed before Petra signaled to change again; however, by the third bath Robert was beginning to enjoy the experience. The water no longer felt cold, but stimulating. His body was becoming numb to the changes, creating the sensation of separating from himself.

Then they entered the *steam room*—a thick blanket of warmth clouded everything, rich with the scent of herbs; cleansing vapors that opened pores and dampened hair. Front-center was a lamp glowing like a beacon in the fog. All one heard was dripping from somewhere in the tepid mist. As if in slow motion, a body appeared and approached a stone basin, the hazy figure reaching inside to take a bucket-full of water and pour it over his head. Robert sat up straight, feeling the warmth in his back, as he attempted to clear his mind and focus on the light, inhaling slowly and deeply as he consumed the herbal fumes. Petra approached the basin and poured some of its water over her body. Without a word, Robert followed suit. The water from the fountain was, like the bath outside, icy-cold, and Robert felt the stinging sensation an infant must feel when it first enters the world.

Once outside the steam room, everything seemed louder and more chaotic than it had before. Jürgen handed Robert a cup and told him to drink from it. Before them was a fountain spewing out steaming water that Robert immediately recognized as that which he often drank from the Kochbrunnen—and the briny draft entered him like milk into a baby. It was amazing to imagine all the natural currents flowing beneath this city, like veins in an organism or roots beneath a tree, connecting it like the metro connects Paris. Robert looked up and noticed there were many people around, and he had to remind himself that they were all naked. Petra tapped him on the back signaling to take another shower before entering the *warm room*. Here they rested for fifteen minutes before entering the *hot room*: a sauna of sorts with a glass wall and wooden lounge chairs to lie on, where another ten minutes passed and Robert felt his strength leave him altogether.

Finally, after another shower, they went to the *quiet room*. It was furnished with lounge chairs and decorated with paneled walls and pictures, giving the impression of being in someone's living room instead of a bathhouse. Robert did not recall in all his experience so comfortable a chair. The frame was made of polished red-brown wood, antique in design though obviously new, and the cushions were covered in a soft cotton material. A cylindrical cushion supported the head; it was attached to the chair with a cord, and could be adjusted to fit snugly behind the base of the neck. Robert let his entire weight onto these cushions with his head cocked back and his arms poised at an unnatural height, laying like deadweights on the wide armrests. It seemed a great effort to glance at his companions who were now laid out like corpses in a morgue; the slightest movement brought a strain to muscles he wouldn't have otherwise realized existed. Processes that usually acted in stealth and mysterious ways were now thrusting within him most palpably. His pulse was thumping in his neck and in his wrists, sweat glands were drying up, and pores were constricting to their normal size.

Upon awakening, he found Jürgen and Petra dressed and ready to go. They were happily snickering, and commented that the baths had had a noticeable affect on him. When the three met up again, after Robert had dressed, they exited the building to find a blanket of snow had transformed the city. All were filled with excitement, and Robert, having grown up in a Mediterranean climate, was particularly inspired.

With heartfelt sincerity he thanked his hosts. Petra reminded him that they had enjoyed themselves no less. Jürgen also put in his two bits and without losing his jovial tone threw in the following message: "I have good news—important news. You're finally invited! I knew it was coming. We'll meet on Thursday, at 9:00 PM, at the main bar in Käfer's. But please, make sure you're on time. Everything is going perfectly. I think," he added, drying his spectacles on a towel, "Italy will be the theme of our New Year's Eve party this year."

Robert did not undervalue the remark. It was of no slight importance to him, for this invitation from a man whom he had never met was clearly a prelude to something more involved than met the eye, and it showed that he had fulfilled a requirement or passed a test. And yet he could not understand how Jürgen could be so casual about so important an invitation, in which this mystery person appealed to a select group to take part in God knew what sort of activities. Jürgen himself had been included in this circle only because of some very special circumstances, to be gone into later, and all this was the reason he took such an interest in Robert to begin with. Nevertheless, the exhaustion from the baths and the beauty of the falling snow made it difficult to judge Jürgen's intonation, and later it was as if the offer was never made.

Chapter XIV

One afternoon, Robert ascended to his attic: up the Neroberg, through the wrought iron gate, past his host family outback in the garden and then up three flights of stairs before reaching his room. This was no small task: even on cold days one broke out in a sweat not midway up the hill and the flights of stairs were steep, particularly the old wooden one up to the attic. During his climb, he thought—as he often did at this moment— how tiresome his life had become; that he had taken such pains to create a lonely existence for himself, abandoning friendships, begging loved ones for the space to move on, severing ties and traveling thousands of miles to a place where no one could reach him; all for the express purpose of hiking up a hill to reach an empty room in someone else's house. While at the same time other ghosts in him gloried at the fact that he was alone, making it on his own and relishing the adventure of leaving the world behind. Indeed, it seemed there was nothing worse than losing this independence.

Churning these thoughts over and over in his mind, still breathing heavily from the walk, Robert dozed off under the last light of day. When he awoke, all he could see were the glowing red numbers of his clock, which happened to be turning from 19:11 to 19:12. After a moment of lethargy, from out of nowhere a swell of panic filled his chest as a voice from within suddenly announced that it was Friday: the evening he was supposed to meet Monika!

The following forty-five minutes needn't be described in detail; but, suffice it to say, despite no little expenditure of energy (and a less than perfect hairdo) Robert made it to his date on time. Upon arriving, he took a seat at the bar and ordered a Calvados. Next to him a couple was speaking quietly, but intensely, the man dressed in a suit and tie, his date wearing jeans. There was a candle between them and an empty bottle of wine. The bartender brought the Calvados along with a candle and some nuts. Robert toasted himself and took a sip, but scarcely had the glass left his lips when he felt two fair hands cover his eyes accompanied by a lovely voice asking him to "guess who?"

"No Jokes," he said, pulling Monika's hands from his face. "Not until you tell me the secret. Otherwise, I won't speak to you."

"Do you promise?" she asked, taking a tube of lipstick from her purse.

Robert wasn't amused.

"We're driving to Frankfurt," she told him, "to see a play. Okay? And I hope you appreciate that it was very difficult to get the tickets. My friend at the office got them, and it took all my charms to make him give them up."

"I love a resourceful woman."

"Don't you know? I always get what I want."

"Me too, as long as I'm not paying," Robert said—or some such words. Moreover, this was true: he should have held his tongue, but it was already too late. Her blue eyes fixed on him, and then a smirk appeared on the corner of her lips: "By the way," she said, "I'll have a Caipirinha. I hope you've not forgotten you're paying tonight." Naturally, Robert saw the message in her quip. This was not the type of woman who enjoyed being manipulated. He weaseled his way around it, however, with a joke about the superior quality of the soda pop at this place. If he was paying, then why not for something cheap.

"You're a funny man," she said, motioning to the bartender to fix her drink. "Sometimes I think I know you, and other times not at all. If you don't mind my saying, it's like you're hiding something."

The problem with intelligent women is that they ask simple questions. Naïve people want to hear about philosophy, history and psychology; sharp ones want to hear the truth. "Please don't say that," he pleaded, "I want you to know me, really. And if I am hiding something, it seems to be from myself, as well." Then he paused. "Maybe you can help me. We have a game in America; it's called 'Truth or Dare'."

She didn't seem to understand.

"It's easy," he said. "We ask each other questions, and must swear on our honor, on the blood of our ancestors, that we answer them with the 'truth.' The promise is extremely serious to us, and nobody breaks the rules—ever. It might sound strange, but it's true. And because this rule may never be broken, we have a way out. Rather than answering the question, which can sometimes be embarrassing, we can choose to take a 'dare'— some sort of action that the question-asker thinks up, like touch your finger to your nose, or kiss the girl across from you on the lips."

"I think I know this game. We call it—"

"Great, shall I begin?"

"Wait!" she protested, "You're the one who needs help. I'll go first, thank you." Robert feigned innocence, but she was playing it tough. "This means I can ask any question I wish, correct? And you must tell me the truth."

"I promise," he said, holding his fingers in the air like a scout.

"This is not easy. So... Have you ever had a German girlfriend before?"

It was an admirable opening move, and Robert duly nodded his respect. He looked her squarely in the eyes and waited, assessing her every movement, observing her breathing and noting the frequency of her blinks, like a gladiator summing up his opponent before the bout. At length he responded: "Yes."

"Now that's interesting! And do—"

"Okay, my turn. How old were you the first time you went to bed with a boy? And I mean all the way."

The scene was not without humor: the chic blonde lost her grin, started biting her lip and stuck her hand in the wine reaching for some peanuts. Her cheeks had flared with color, and her eyes expressed sincere fret. "I'm not going to answer that question!" Her voice was trembling. "I can't believe you asked me that!"

"Would you like to take a dare instead?" he coolly rejoined, gloating over his virtuoso strategy. Indeed, whether Monika was a fiery nymphet or a late bloomer was unimportant. His intent was not to make a point, but to observe his date. She was aghast.

"Shall we stop the game?" Robert asked.

"Yes, we'll stop this...I was 21, okay. I know it's late...I wanted it to be special, that's all. You can understand that, can't you?"

"Your turn."

She was clearly struggling. "Do all Americans play this way?"

"Is that your question?"

"Okay, I'm learning," she said, tucking a wisp of hair behind her ear. "So, look at me now. Look at my body. If you could touch any part of me, even for a moment, which part would you choose first?"

Robert gave her a long and measuring stare. "Your heart."

She laughed. "Now I know you can't be trusted!"

"All right," he said, clasping his hands and bringing out the heavy artillery, "when was the last time you went to bed with a man? Remember, no lies."

The ploy worked beautifully, causing Monika to make a loud gulp. A kind of ecstatic apprehension, if it may be put this way, was suddenly apparent in every feature of her face; so much so, in fact, that Robert felt ill at ease. To her credit she didn't give up; and after a few moments of deliberation, she opted for the untested and titillating "dare."

"So you don't want to talk, do you?" Robert blurted accusingly, losing his composure under the knowledge that his opponent had a secret. "All right," he said, rolling up his sleeves, "I want you to put both your hands on my chest and tell me, in German, that you want to sleep with *me* tonight." His intonation on the word "me" betrayed a comparison with another, probably nonexistent, man. Retaining control during such games is not apparent.

All of sudden Monika passionately seized her date, squeezing him tightly and clawing at his sweater, bringing her lips seductively near to his. What she said, Robert would never know, but the couple sitting next to them practically bumped heads as they turned to see what was happening. Robert did his best to regain his faculties, telling his date that he didn't know what she said, but he "sure did like it." Monika asked him if that was enough, leaving Robert to ponder something beautiful, at which point he affirmed that her performance was more than satisfactory.

"Okay, next question," she said, taking Robert's hand. "Do you want me to be your girlfriend?"

"I—what?"

"You heard me. I want to know what your feelings are. And if you take this game seriously like you say, then you should tell me the truth right now. I think I like the idea of not having to wonder if you're interested in me only for my 'heart'." She leaned forward as she spoke.

"I—" he glanced down for a moment, "but, that's not fair. Two minutes ago you refused to tell me the last time you went to bed with another man!"

Just as Robert was about to break down and throw a good old fashioned temper tantrum, divine inspiration struck in the form of the infamous "dare" option. Of course, as an experienced player and patriot of the nation that never grows up, he recognized the risks involved, especially when engaging in a public place. Nevertheless, he tightened his belt buckle, mustered up some courage and dropped the word on his date. To his credit, it took her a few moments to come up with the right challenge to get what she wanted from her indecisive man. The bad news is that he would have been better off holding with his "truth" when the command was given: "I want you to kiss me," she said with an expressly devilish smile, "on the lips, and for at least thirty seconds. I'll have the answer to my question one way or another."

Some readers may be thinking that Robert is a lucky man: he is. Nevertheless this sudden turn of events stunned him. Indeed, for some time he had wanted to kiss her, much more than that if we're to be honest, and he had even dreamt of it the night before their date. Earlier that day he was craving her touch, pining for her body, tingling from head to toe with naughty anticipation; but now there was fear. Her control over the situation caught him off guard—it was like being exposed, an involuntary letting of the truth. Sharing the truth is one thing; revealing it is quite another. And there was no time to think! It was not like in a book where one can stop the clock and describe a scene with artificial detail.

He brought his lips to hers and let them touch. He lost himself in her—the smell of her skin, the softness of her hair. It felt heavenly to be close; sharing what could only be the germ of a deep and lasting love.

Chapter XV

"But this couldn't possibly be the meeting place of a club," Robert thought, as he hung his coat on the stand. Upon entering the establishment, by way of two sets of glass-paned doors, one was met with a massive oak bar; behind which were no less than four tenders clad in white collared shirts, black bow ties and aprons like waiters in a Parisian café. Near the corner was an ebony grand piano, on top of which was an exceptionally gaudy candelabrum. Its player was dressed in a tuxedo, wearing round glasses with tortoise-shell rims, and tickling the ivory to the tune of something jazzy. Robert could hear him singing to himself and recognized he was American. He was also the only black man in the place.

Around the piano were couples feigning musical appreciation. One man, dressed in a blue suit with gold cufflinks and a silk handkerchief, was pretending to sing into an invisible microphone while unsuccessfully attempting to keep rhythm with a spoon. There was a bevy of women at the bar. One of these ladies, possessing an uncanny resemblance to a tapir, was excitedly waving her serviette to a gentleman at the far end of the restaurant. He pretended not to notice. And was it a woman who decorated the place with at least 200 pictures of the Eiffel Tower? You couldn't move without catching another view of it. It was more difficult avoiding it here than from the Trocadero in Paris!

With a familiar tap on the shoulder, Robert turned to greet his friend with a question about "Green Fairies." Leaning against the back of the bar was a chalkboard with the cocktail of the evening artistically advertised. Today it was called "La Fée Verte".

Jürgen giggled, playfully pushed Robert and held out his hand letting his pinky dangle flimsily. He did his best to imitate the accent of a flamboyant queen, if one can imagine a straight-laced German doing this. "Aren't you too old to ask these questions?"

"I mean the cocktail," Robert said, rolling his eyes.

Jürgen was obviously disappointed that Robert didn't break out laughing. He shrugged his shoulders and said: "By the looks of that board, I'd say it's the drink of the day—why?"

"Do you know what it stands for? It's Absinthe!"

"Absinthe?" Jürgen repeated, eyeing the chalkboard again and nodding. "Oh yes. Will you have one?"

Now it was Robert who was disappointed: "You don't seem very surprised."

"That's Käfer's," Jürgen said with an odd smile.

"That's impossible!" Robert pleaded. "It's been outlawed since World War I!"

Jürgen nodded his agreement, but then was distracted by a lady in a sequined dress waving the bartender over for more champagne.

"And I must admit," Robert went on, rather miffed with his

friend's disinterest, "I really don't get how relaxed you are about it."

"This is not a normal place," Jürgen explained, "the sooner you learn that the better." And he signaled to the bartender it was time to drink. Robert shrugged his shoulders and, giving in to the absurdity of the moment, ordered a Green Fairy. At the far end of the bar stood a man, approximately 60 years old and fat, pawing a woman no older than 25 and strikingly attractive if one didn't look closely. With an excited nudge, Jürgen explained that the man was none other than Rolf Steinbauer, a television star from the seventies, known most of all for his role as the Munich detective Clemens Starck; his date was Ute Hahn, daughter of Ursula Hahn, a local prominent who supposedly owned four boutiques on the Wilhelmsstrasse.

Suddenly a well-dressed but terribly made up woman broke out crying as the result of a cigarette burn to her white leather purse, though the sobs couldn't distract her colleague who was in the depths of concentration applying a fresh coat of lipstick. She turned to the culprit and said (in terrible-sounding English) "I'm sorry, but in Germany we look where we're standing!"

Only now did Robert notice the culprit was wearing tennis shoes. She turned back to the well-dressed but terribly made up woman and gave a big smile. "Honey, are you talking to me?" she said (in perfect American English).

"*Scheisse!*" said the well-dressed woman (in perfect German).

The American understood and promptly turned her back on

the angry lady; but before the scene had come to a close, the bartender returned with a candle, a bowl of peanuts and two cocktails. He bowed his head and addressed the two young men as "Messieurs" while sliding the glasses toward them with his fingertips. Robert took a sip of his drink and suddenly broke out laughing. It's true, he thought; there was something special about this place; and, as these thoughts were passing through his mind, he was met with the view of a peculiar man.

It was an older fellow; with frazzled gray hair, a pointed beard, and a distinctively aquiline nose that drew one's attention to his unusual countenance. In short, the guy looked like a hybrid of a mad scientist and the devil himself. And yet there was something familiar about him; something eminently mischievous beaconed from his eyes, as if he were an old friend masquerading as a stranger. Robert was struck firstly by his odd appearance, and secondly by the fact he was fast approaching. All at once the peculiar chap seized Jürgen's hand, making a bizarre shake, and said something in German; and then Jürgen said something in German, and then the man took a step back, looked at Robert and belted out a robust laugh. Jürgen turned to Robert, introducing the man as Herr Eberhard; and then he explained in English that Robert was from America.

The old man burst with glee, seizing Robert's hand and putting his other arm around Robert's shoulders: "America!" he cried, "a wondrous land, sacred land, the rich soil that yielded the brood of Franklin and Washington! The cream of the crop! Eye of the pyramid! The labor of a hundred—what am I saying?—a *thousand* European years condensed into one colossal edifice: the skyscraper! I was lucky. Yes, I admit it. The forests of Penn were my domain: the Keystone State upon which rests the industry of the North and the agriculture of the South. Take it away and the union collapses, as the temple upon the arch. Yes, I ascended the heights of Mount Washington and gazed down upon the confluence of the three majestic rivers. Yes, I stepped beneath the vaults of the Cathedral of Learning, and traced the path of the fortification that bequeathed its name to this proud city: Pittsburgh! Yes, life took sail and I boarded it! And like the three princes of Serendip, I discovered this Shangri-La quite accidentally. So, my boy, are you also a repetitist?"

Robert was dumbfounded. He simply didn't know what to say to this absurdly verbose man before him. As a matter of fact, he was so bowled over by the oratory that he didn't notice his mouth was hanging open. He forced his lips into a smile and scratched his head (with his left hand, his right still being pinioned by the old man). In the end Jürgen answered for him, explaining this was his first time to the special bar. To this Herr Eberhard released Robert and hollered joyously: "By Jove, we've got one!" He spoke in a resonant, well-trained voice. Every word was brimming with personality, drawing attention from anyone who happened to overhear. How this man could rally an audience! And then he grabbed Robert's shoulder again, shaking it furiously. "He looks like he has the makings of one though, if I may offer my prognosis. I daresay a proclivity to it. I can smell it." He sniffed the air, stroked his pointy beard, and then of his own accord took Robert's glass and gave it a swirl: "So what are you doing in Germany, lad? You're not here to learn the language, are you?"

"To be honest—" Robert started, and then the old man interrupted with "How could you be sure?"—"I'm not sure, or what I mean to say"—here he turned to Jürgen and smiled— "is that I haven't—"Of course you haven't!" Herr Eberhard broke in again, this time blocking altogether Robert's train of thought, because apparently the excitement was too much to bear; the old man practically took off: "I knew it!" he cried, "A Knight through and through! Eager to set forth on the path of the adept! Indeed, it's difficult for the polyhistor to find his place in a world imploding at an exponential rate. He inevitably mirrors the artifacts he seeks to learn about." Then he grinned and bent forward as he leaned against the bar, coming close and whispering as if someone were to listen in. "And I ask you, boy; is it merely coincidence that 'wondering' and 'wandering' differ by one letter?"

Robert smiled: that pained, sympathetic grin we make when we suspect someone is nuts. In fact, he began to intuit that more than a few bats were nesting in the belfry of Herr Eberhard, who seemed to have problems knowing when to quit. Without warning, the old man held out his cane, waved it before Robert's face and said: "Take heed of my words, boy. Make no attempt to impede your flight!" His voice was teetering on the edge of a plea. "Perfect enlightenment approaches! Accelerate!"

"But one needs gas to accelerate," Robert contested, examining the cane, the stock of which was black, and the handle carved ivory in the shape of an Egyptian sarcophagus. On his wrinkled, but refined looking hand was a gold ring; the kind one uses to seal a letter.

"To be, or not to be," Herr Eberhard quoted, holding one hand firmly over his heart (the one with the cane) and extending the other dramatically in the air to three ladies by the piano, "that is the question!" He actually got a smile out of one, and a drunk in the corner started to clap. "Transcend this nature that binds you to reflection! Act! Stop waiting! And must you employ such a crude analogy?"

"I'm sorry; I'm feeling a bit—"

"The forty-nine days have begun!" cheered the old man, bringing his crescendo to a histrionic climax. And with this he bowed his head, clicked his heels, and shook the hands of the two young men, again and again, shaking their arms violently and repeatedly thanking them for their time. Then he speedily made his exit, vanishing through a door in the back of the restaurant. Jürgen commented on how much time Herr Eberhard had given them. Robert could only ask how long his friend had known this character.

"I can't remember," he replied, sipping his whiskey. "It must be here at Käfer's that we met. It's always here that we meet. I know Herr Eberhard is crazy, but don't judge him. He is not like other people. He's somehow better. Really, I wish I could thank him for all that he has given me. He's opened my eyes to truths I still don't believe! Anyway, his conversation is always entertaining, and you must respect that."

"True," Robert admitted, "a subject's only as interesting as the person describing it."

Jürgen patted Robert on the back and laughed. "Who cares if he wears his hat backwards!"

"But Jürgen, what were these words he used? Within minutes he dubbed me with no less than two labels."

"As for the word 'polyhistor', I never heard it before in my life. But that's typical for Herr Eberhard. He makes up words often and it's difficult to know what is in the dictionary or not. As for the word 'repetitist', this I know. It's his favorite word."

"And what in the name of God is a 'repetitist'?" Robert demanded.

Jürgen took another sip of his drink, looked around the bar and then nonchalantly continued: "Herr Eberhard argues that during the normal span of events which make up a human life, we can tap into but one great thought at best. And the secret to intellectual development is to repeat that thought as much as possible."

"You're sounding as weird as him!"

"Well, it's not my fault! So Herr Eberhard's one great thought in life is called 'Diachronic Repetition'."

"Please continue," Robert implored, holding his drink up to the light and giving it a shake.

"According to Herr Eberhard," Jürgen explained, emphasizing that the theory was not his own, "Diachronic Repetition is the process by which we repeat events with the goal of blending them into a single memory, or something like that. For instance, I'm coming here to Käfer's at the same time, on the same day and drinking the same drink for at least three years. I admit this is all thanks to Herr Eberhard. The result is that my brain can no longer remember the individual evenings. And believe it or not, as I speak to you now, I have no idea of time; only the addition of you to my mental picture of this bar."

"You seem to enjoy it."

"Herr Eberhard believes it's the secret to appreciate life at the deepest levels. Sometimes he repeats conversations we had months, even years earlier, word for word. Even tonight, I'm sure I heard that one about the skyscraper before. When he speaks, his voice echoes in my memory."

Such was Jürgen's discrete way of making an indiscretion: if he had known better, he wouldn't have said too much about Herr Eberhard, and yet his innate sense of jurisprudence enabled him to share the little secrets of his liaison with the old man, as only a person who knows how to keep the big secrets can be.

Robert didn't notice. "I must admit," he said, gulping down his milky-green concoction and smacking his lips, "I've always been the type to seek out a neighborhood hangout, rather than everyday a new café. And I like it when I don't have to order my espresso when I sit down—you know, these 'Green Fairies' are good."

"Perhaps Herr Eberhard doesn't know reality," concluded Jürgen with a melancholic smile, "but he reads people well."

Robert looked across the bar. The piano player was aimlessly tinkling away. During the last twenty minutes it was as if the music had been turned off. Even the noise of the crowd had faded. But now the roar was back, the uncontrolled laughter, clinking glasses, humming chatter, clapping hands and a raspy cough coming from near the shellfish buffet. On top of that, there seemed to be even more women than earlier; and they seemed to be getting older to boot. Most of the men had exhausted themselves and had escaped to their suburban homes. The ones remaining were too inebriated to pay attention to anyone else but themselves. Jürgen took the last sip of his drink and said nothing. Robert watched the piano player who now had a beauty teetering next to him, a real kurort queen, whose hindered equilibrium appeared graceful in the music.

Jürgen smiled, rattling the ice cubes of his empty glass: "Let's eat this week up," he said. "Eat it in one bite. You don't even need to call. Just show up at the bar."

Chapter XVI

What had begun as an incidental discovery was developing into a full-blown monomania: the conviction that a profound change was occurring within him, in conjunction with a burning curiosity as to the mechanisms of that change, was consuming Robert's every thought. And the key appeared to lie within the water. He no longer missed a day without visiting one of Wiesbaden's sources at least once. In fact, he began to discover more, hidden among the gables and turrets of the old city center, with strange, unwieldy names like Bäckerbrunnen, Faulbrunnen and Schützenhofquelle. This last fountain, which means "Archery Court Source," was during Roman times sheltered by a temple dedicated to the Celtic goddess of healing Sirona. Today its water surfaces between a bakery and clothing store, and, like the Kochbrunnen, its flavor is salty. On one occasion, Robert partook of the springs no less than five times in one afternoon. Something was compelling him to learn more about this liquid that brought the ancients here. Mounted next to the fountains were plaques providing a chemical analysis of the water. At the Kochbrunnen, which Robert considered strongest of the sources, the composition was remarkably complex, containing no less than fifteen elements ranging from Ammonia to Strontium. Robert recorded in a notebook all the relevant information, quantities and statistics.

The following table is a facsimile of the chart found at the Kochbrunnen, and identical to the version Robert painstakingly copied, letter for letter, into his notebook:

Heilwasseranalyse Trinkstelle "Kochbrunnen"
Quantitative Chemische Untersuchung

Kationen	(mg/l)
Lithium (Li)	3,3
Natrium (Na)	2.625
Kalium (K)	88,0
Ammonium (NH4)	5,4
Magnesium (Mg)	47,0
Calcium (Ca)	341
Strontium (Sr)	15,3
Mangan (Mn)	0,38
Eisen (Fe)	2,8
Anionen	
Flourid (F)	0,59
Chlorid (Cl)	4.530
Bromid (Br)	4,1
Sulfat (SO4)	68,9
Hydrogenarsenat (HAsO4)	0,20
Hydrogencarbonat (HCO3)	567

At the top of the list was lithium, a potentially toxic substance used in the treatment of manic-depression. That struck Robert as curious. Many users become dependent on it, and if his memory hadn't failed him, hydrogen arsenate, coming from arsenic, is a poison. Fluoride is good for your teeth and calcium is good for your bones. Chloride is a binary compound of chlorine, which is a highly irritating, greenish-yellow gaseous element used as a disinfectant, a bleaching agent, and in making chloroform. Below the list was a warning stating in bold red print that no more than a liter per day should be drunk. None of it made sense. People had been coming here for thousands of years with good results, and yet this description sounded like a Molotov cocktail!

Robert sipped the steaming draft and watched the condensation exit his mouth, these crisp winter days being perfect for the consumption of his "medicine." He re-examined his notes. Yes, a mineral composition: this esoteric puzzle that had yet to reveal itself. Indeed, during the previous months of regular consumption, the flavor of the water had clearly changed. The first time you taste it, the flavor is quite foreign, the experience unpleasant. What follows, however, could be described as a metamorphosis of taste. At the beginning, you notice the salt. This phase lasts for some time and is typified by a neutral relationship between the drinker and the liquid. Later, you notice a metallic aftertaste, and eventually you're struck with the sensation that there is an egg in the water. It's at this moment that the drinker realizes the flavor he tastes is rich and complex. This is the beginning of appreciation. As with a piece of good music, one discovers a myriad of tone and pitch at first undetected; and like the amateur of music, the amateur of water sets out to identify and appreciate not only the finished composition, but also the elements that form the whole. As Robert examined his notes, he attempted to distinguish each of the minerals passing across his tongue.

The discomfort in the lower back had been acting up again; not a pain to call a doctor about, but a reminder. It was

Wednesday, 10:45, and as Robert put away his cup and headed up the Taunusstrasse, he thought about the similarity between this day and the many other Wednesdays he had now spent here. Something strange was happening. He was no longer dividing his time chronologically by the week, but categorically by the day of the week. He wasn't thinking of what he had done the previous week or a fortnight ago, but what he did on "Wednesdays" or "Thursdays." About half way up the street, he passed the Parsival, but then continued, beyond the shops, slowly rising above the city.

Chapter XVII

With a clap of the hands the teacher called out the word "*Akkusativ*" and Robert felt a lump form in his throat. The past weeks had not been the most productive regarding the linguistic development of the man who came to Germany to learn German. By the expressions on their faces, one could see which students had been speaking German and which had been lapping up too much spa water; most had a healthy look of concentration, with the exception of Robert who was making the expression of a goldfish.

After class he met Nermina in the hall and asked her how

she was doing. "Me?" she said, putting both hands on her belly. "Fat! If I eat another one of those gingerbread cookies, I'm going to pop."

"And Radovan?" he asked. "Is he still hard at work solving the problems of the world?"

She answered with a grunt. "I rarely see him from all his contemplating. Ah, but you're in luck this evening; Belgrade's philosopher is coming to pick me up."

Radovan appeared at the end of the hall. He was wearing a wool overcoat and long gray scarf, green cords and boots that Oliver Twist would have turned down. If one didn't know any better, one would have taken him for a Bohemian—a Bohemian farmer. His pants were frayed at the seams. His scarf was stained with coffee. The gloves he was wearing were not only threadbare, but torn in several places, something Robert couldn't help noticing, and yet this raggedy outfit lent him a kind of dignity; he wore it well and the look agreed with his uprooted existence.

The burly man greeted his wife with a kiss and Robert with a wise crack about California's civil war; and no sooner had the chuckles subsided, he was demanding they all find the nearest watering hole. Robert suggested a nearby piano bar and the trio was on its way. After a short walk, they arrived to find the place busy, but not full. In the corner, beneath a wooden statue of Saint Peter, was a free table. Nermina took a Riesling, Robert a glass of Bordeaux.

"And what is 'Mr. Philosophy' having this evening?" queried Nermina.

"Good question, dear wife," he said, holding his finger in the air. "Vodka, cold and pure—like a drop from the ice that saved mother Russia."

"In other words, the usual," she moaned, ordering the drinks while Radovan discussed the crystal liquor's origin. He proclaimed that its name came from the Slavic word *voda*, meaning water. *Vodka* meant *little water*, which in Radovan's opinion was cute. It was the perfect thing for a "little thirst." Then he added that it was 800 years old and came from Poland. Robert thought that the drink came from Russia and suspected that it could be much older.

Nermina, frustrated with the pedantic vein of this dispute, couldn't resist adding her two bits: "I'm not sure what the two of you are arguing about? As you know them, neither Russia nor Poland existed 800 years ago. It's essentially the same region you're talking about."

"You're right," conceded Robert. "We're talking about people, not land."

"More than that," added Radovan, "we're talking about movements of people."

The drinks arrived and Robert made a toast "to movements of people."

The three drank, making sure to look each other in the eye as they clinked glasses. Robert took a sip and smacked his lips. Nermina said "cheers" and then, in a most discerning manner, reminiscent of an enologist passing judgment, she tested the wine's bouquet, commented on its body and then sipped it, savoring its subtle flavor as one whose soul had been lit afire. Radovan knocked back his Vodka in a single gulp and then burped.

"My friend," he said, wiping his mouth and looking Robert squarely in the eyes, "do you know what an exodus is?"

"Of course," Robert answered, "it's a movement of people."

"It's a one-way trip—a voyage; and it's an aspect of human nature carried out since the origins of our existence."

"Then it must bring us good," Robert concluded.

The Yugoslavian laughed. "Only to those who walk!" and then, slapping Robert on the back, he went on making remarks about other topics. He was convinced that immigrants made the world go round. Sedentary folk, he claimed, were nothing more than "bushes on the landscape." People who didn't leave their birthplace were doomed to supporting roles in the great theater of life. "Real Parisians?" he asked as if speaking to himself. Real Parisians were stuck in banks and bakeries. The people who make Paris famous, the ones who create the myths, none of them, he argued, were born there. As he talked, he kept prodding Robert on the shoulder, asking for his agreement. Robert forced himself to answer, but what he was really thinking about was Käfer's. What did Herr Eberhard mean by forty-nine days? Perfect enlightenment? There was definitely something wrong with that old man: But what? And on second thought, it was presumptuous of Jürgen to plan the next meeting without asking first. Anyway, it felt good to be talking with Radovan and Nermina. Why is it we are attracted to nuts and loons when it's normal people who possess all the wisdom?

Chapter XVIII

Robert entered the café, panting from his trek back down the hill, to find the place empty. The bartender greeted him with a nod and a look to suggest he could choose any table he wished. He took a seat near the window and about ten minutes later Petra arrived at which point he greeted her with two kisses on the cheeks, and thanks for the rendezvous. She reminded him that he was also to be thanked; this was one of those days when she just couldn't make the trip to Frankfurt.

Robert, of course, was impelled to ask: "And what is it you do in Frankfurt?"

"Sshh, don't tell anyone," she whispered. "It's my greatest secret. I work, a little bit, not everyday, but enough. I work with my parents."

"And what do your parents do?" he asked.

"My father is in banking."

"Well," Robert rejoined, furtively glancing to and fro, as if to assure the top-secret nature of this conversation, "I promise not to tell anyone as long as you promise not to tell that I don't work."

The two shook hands; Petra crossed her heart and gave Robert a smile. He ordered an espresso, she a cappuccino, and no sooner had the waiter turned around, Robert asked what was burning inside him: he had to know if Petra was familiar with Herr Eberhard.

She raised her eyebrows. "So you've been to Käfer's, have you?"

"You do know him!" exclaimed Robert.

"Take my advice, stay away from that kook." She began nervously stirring her coffee. "And especially, don't believe a word he says. He's crazy, you know. I already warned you. Remember?"

"Well, he did seem a bit odd."

"A bit odd?" Her brown eyes began to bulge. "He's stark, raving mad!" And before Robert could get a word in edgewise, she demanded that he describe the visit to Käfer's.

Thus Robert recounted his conversation with Herr Eberhard and Jürgen, emphasizing the bit about the old man's trip to the states and leaving out the parts about "Diachronic Repetition" and "Perfect Enlightenment" so as not to clutter his narrative with excessive detail; but, above all, because in the presence of Petra he felt a certain degree of shame.

"And you believe old crafty-lips has been to America?"

"Why shouldn't I?" Robert replied.

"He's supposedly a retired *Gymnasium* instructor, you know."

"A fitness instructor?"

"No silly, *Gymnasium* is the German equivalent of your American high school; only with more thinking and fewer cheerleaders."

"And what did he teach?" Robert persisted.

"Not how to dress!" she affirmed, and then broke out laughing. "No one knows. Actually, no one knows where he's from. He's not from Wiesbaden. I'd say he's not from this world." Robert smiled. He knew he shouldn't have done this and yet her seriousness gave him the giggles. She promptly changed her tone: "You think it's funny, don't you. You're just like Jürgen. But, if it makes you feel any better, I think you should know that 'Eberhard' isn't even the old phony's name. That's a lie too. Try looking him up in the phone book. His real name is 'Thödol' or something of the like. I found it on a piece of paper in Jürgen's wallet one night after he fell asleep. What I'm trying to say is that nobody really knows who he is, and as far as I'm concerned that's dangerous."

"Well, Herr Eberhard or Thödol or whatever his name is"— (Eberhard was easier to pronounce)—"did have some interesting ideas about lifestyle, and lately I've noticed that things often repeat."

She shrugged. "I know, I know, Jürgen enjoys talking with him, too. I know." (Jürgen was probably the type to describe every meeting in detail.) "What I don't know is how you can handle that brain-splitting lack of logic for longer than a minute.

Ah, but Jürgen just loves it. Within all that pomposity and empty chatter, my boyfriend thinks he's going to find the secret to sloughing off." The look in Petra's eyes bespoke her frustration, as though any form of sympathy for the man was a personal offense. "Do you know what Jürgen calls that pseudo-Masonic fool? 'The Master of the Lodge.' Now if that's not strange, I don't know what is."

"Wait a minute," Robert pleaded. "What do you mean 'Masonic'—now a Freemason? He's not in that secret society, is he?"

"As far as I'm concerned, it's a sect. Didn't you notice the way he shook Jürgen's hand? I think it's creepy. He claims it was the reason he went to 'America' –land of the all-seeing eye, as he likes to put it—but I don't trust the blowhard. He pretends to be mister know-it-all with his cocky light-heartedness and Epicurean savvy, but there's something wrong with him, something sinister."

"Maybe you're right," Robert conceded.

"What do you mean, maybe?" she said, rolling her eyes. "I know I'm right!" And sensing the urgency of Robert's misconception, she decided to drive the point home: "Darling, there are things that people mustn't know. For reasons unknown, we must act on certain thoughts once they're presented to us. They work within us like a challenge, gnawing on our conscience until we can no longer stand the curiosity, and then, like moths to a flame, we try to find out what the light is all about. This is what the Greeks meant by the Sirens' song, the Jews and Christians with their idea of Forbidden Fruit. Simply put, it's knowledge that kills; and it's the stuff Herr Eberhard deals with." Robert smiled, but didn't speak. Her eyes fixed on him pleadingly. "And believe me, that conniving windbag doesn't care who he drags down with him. I wish you hadn't mentioned his name."

Her sincerity was frightening. It demonstrated clearly that philosophizing was no game to Petra; that she bore her convictions with absolute seriousness; and woe betide he who crossed her. The coffee arrived and Robert promptly broke a sugar cube, plopped it in the cup and polished off his espresso in a single sip. Outside it had begun to snow. Petra looked good in this café, seated with legs crossed and playing with a lock of hair. There was so much he wanted to say; so much to confess and explain: "Do you remember the evening we spent together, Petra, the one when we drank the martinis?"

"I thought we'd never speak of this," she replied, gently biting her lip and glancing at Robert's hands.

"I can't help myself," he said. "I mean, I can't help from thinking about some of the things you said."

She looked at him with concern. "What did I say?"

"For one thing, you said life had no meaning."

"Of course," she returned, a smile forming on her face.

"Don't you find that a bit pessimistic?"

To this her smile grew into a giggle: "Not at all, for me it's realistic."

Robert was pained. "But if we can't find any meaning in life, how can we find happiness in it?"

"You are a eudemonist at heart, aren't you? Must everything hold the final result of happiness?"

"Well, for me, yes. But what's a eudemonist?"

"It's a good word," she said, with a charmingly pragmatic intonation, "that's what it is. *Eu* is Greek for good. *Demon* means spirit. Fits you perfectly if I think about it. And it's not one of those terms that senile chatterbox comes up with. It's the philosophy of happiness: that your actions should be judged on their capacity to bring happiness. It sets it as the basis for living—the goal. Are you living for money? For fame? For success, whatever that word means? It's your word, Robert. It's how you live your life."

"This is what I am?"

"Robert," she explained, "life, as I see it, is Nature. The distinction between the blossoming of a flower and that of a girl is slight. Both acts are beautiful in their simplicity. Indeed, to attribute any more meaning to the blossoming of the girl than to that of the flower is to diminish the beauty of the act. I see all life this way. I see it as a singular whole, not as a conglomeration; and to separate humankind from that whole is to divorce it from life itself."

"And therefore you attribute no meaning to Nature."

"Exactly," she returned. "To imagine the waterfall gushes over the precipice for some celestial purpose is to deny its majesty. Why must we constantly attempt to control our environment with our intellect? I mean, no one seems to notice it's a losing battle."

"And how do you control your desire to attach meaning to the events around you?"

"Through aestheticism," she said, taking a sip of her cappuccino. "I seek out the aesthetic value of events, not their symbolic value. To define is to qualify, and to qualify is to restrict; and if I'm to restrict the events around me, I'm to deny myself the chance to fully appreciate their aesthetic value."

"So you do see life as beautiful," Robert concluded.

"As beautiful as death," she said.

He smiled curiously, gazing into her intelligent brown eyes, and wondered what kind of a person was behind them. Had her childhood really been so different than his? What makes a European European? Even in repose, she exuded a gravity foreign to younger lands.

"By the way," she said. "If I hadn't kicked you out that night, just how far would you have gone?"

"How far did we go?"

"Really, so silly," she mused, shaking her head and crushing with her spoon the sugar left at the bottom of her cup. "And Robert," she added with a distinct change in tone, "please remember what I said. Don't let your curiosity get the better of you, stay away from that old humbug. It's possible you're already a part of some devious plan. Nothing's haphazard with him. If he chose to meet you, it's for some demented purpose, I'm sure. Believe me, he'll pull the wool over your eyes, spin you around three times and lead you up the garden path before you know what hit you. He's a fake, a cheat and a charlatan; and he's much more dangerous than you realize. I can't make it any clearer than that. I'm serious. Please, don't talk to him anymore."

"Okay, Petra."

"Promise me, Robert."

"I promise."

Chapter XIX

After skimming some fifty words with the prefix poly, he came upon it: *polyhistor*—coming from *polus* (much) and *histor* (learned), a polymath. A few lines down was polymath: one of great or varied learning. Robert noted the Greek roots of this word, and recalled how Germans pronounce the letter "y" like an English "u." He thought of the term "Renaissance Man"— Leonardo da Vinci, someone who could paint a masterpiece and dissect a corpse with the same skill and grace, someone who could speak of the immensity of the universe and the minuteness of an atom in the same breath; and, as he thought about this word, he became moved that Herr Eberhard had used it in reference to him. True, Robert's one wish in life was the acquisition of a diverse and voluminous knowledge. This was the first time anyone had recognized him for that. It was also the first time a title had been given to the feeling that had burned for so long in his heart. Jürgen was right; this peculiar man had the gift of reading people.

Robert shut the dictionary and put it on the nightstand. Then he grabbed the phone and dialed; and as soon as Monika heard his voice, hers lifted. His followed suit: "I'm afraid," he uttered in his most cavalier tone, "I have a grave problem that only you can help me with. You see this evening is my German class and—" This was all it took to elicit a seductively positive response, as well as her address. And really, he thought grabbing his coat, what a stroke of luck she was at home with nothing to do.

He headed down the Taunusstrasse, enjoying its proud architecture, and stopped at the Kochbrunnen for a drink. At first he felt a chill of anxiety run down his spine, but the salty, piping-hot nectar quickly effected its spell. Once the fluid had entered his body, it traveled to the lower regions of his back. Then, as more water came, the energy cumulated. There was a gradual increase in temperature and then, as incredible as this all sounds, the aqueous warmth began to mount up the spine like mercury in a thermometer. By the time it reached the head, gushing into the brain through the back of the skull, the sensation was so intense it could only be described as boiling. Like a violent eruption, all was burning as his head fell back and his vision faded to a blur of sparkling red and yellow, exploding in his mind to a state of rapt hydrophilia.

For an instant he was struck with guilt: the desire to imbibe this questionable remedy seemed wrong. Was it not, in fact, flirting with obsession—or, worse yet, admitting to an illness? And (yes, this was the key, beyond all shadow of doubt) to resign to this curiosity, antisocial by its discomfiture, was to yield to a natural inclination for a solitary life. But then, as Robert traversed the quiet streets, and the salty warmth in him cooled, he thought about Monika again, and the Philharmonie and the last time they were there. His behavior was not particularly normal; and come to think of it, she never said whether she liked his kiss or not. It was one of those moments when he came up with an idea that took him where he didn't want to go with the result of precisely reaching the goal for which he had originally hoped. And, if that little adventure wasn't enough, he had now decided to thrust himself into a new one where he may well be forced to explain!

Above the entrance to Luxemburgstrasse 6, in bold italic script, was the Latin word *Salve*. Robert examined the panel and found the name Wieland about halfway down. He pressed the button and, without an answer, the front door buzzed itself open. Monika lived on the top floor, there was no lift, and the staircase was steep. Upon reaching her flat, he saw that her door had been cracked, emitting a warm, inviting glow from within.

Her apartment was sparse. The largest piece of furniture was the couch, made from soft black leather. Hanging on the wall above it was a stark, abstract painting, linear like a Mondrian with blotches of red and blue; next to it was a palm with fronds large enough to hang overhead. Monika was tucked in a corner of her couch with book in hand and a glass of wine before her on the coffee table. She told Robert she was glad he came.

He smiled. "Me, too." He approached her and sat on the floor with his elbow propped on the cushion. "You're always around at the best times."

"So," she said, curling her toes beneath her socks, "have you seen any good movies lately?"

As if per order, she extinguished his fear; and no sooner had Robert began to ramble on about seeing Gert Fröbe (known to most Americans as Auric Goldfinger) for the first time in his native tongue, Monika segued into a lecture on directors in Germany. It wasn't long before Cupid had unloaded his entire quiver on Robert who couldn't hold back from sharing how much he loved women who knew film.

She smiled girlishly and looked away: the kind of expression one makes when caught off guard by a compliment with which one agrees: "You're full of praise tonight, aren't you."

"It's true. I consider you the cultural expert of Wiesbaden." This wasn't entirely true: Robert had a habit of misplacing his lust, exaggerating to a fault and showering women with compliments in lieu of molesting them. He considered her beautiful, and, in the fine art of flirtation, one well-placed compliment is worth ten credentials.

She laughed. "I'm bored, that's all."

"That may be, but not boring; and that's what counts."

"Your compliments are driven."

"It's due to their sincerity. You know I think highly of you—ever since I saw you in the Café Parsival. I used to call you the Hollywood star; did I ever tell you? I can still see you there, sitting in that peculiar chair. You were with some other people, as well. But it's funny; I can no longer remember what they looked like. Monika, you're a very special person to me."

Robert was in top form and Monika appeared to be tickled pink with his confession, for she spoke with a naughty smirk on her lips: "And why did you call me the Hollywood star?"

"I honestly don't know," he affirmed. "I think it was the chair; wicker body, fluffy cushion and that particular green and white striped awning attached to it."

She giggled. "You're so funny. Those chairs come from the seaside resorts of North Germany. We call them 'strand baskets'. They have nothing to do with America."

"But why me? What made you choose to smile at me?"

"I noticed you," she said calmly, "because you looked different. Perhaps it was the line of your lips or the shape of your mouth or the way you ran your fingers through your hair. I could see you weren't from here."

Robert hesitantly rose to his feet, glanced at Monika, then at her apartment, and walked to the window. He gazed down onto the street—a man strolled by under a street lamp—and thought about what she had just said; and then, looking out the window, he pondered the catastrophic mistake he had made by quitting university and coming to Germany. He spoke without turning to look at her: "Am I really so different?"

"Maybe I'm also 'out of place,'" she said. "I'm sure a lot of us are. And when we meet each other, there's something sexy about it. We speak in a secret language. I knew you were looking for change."

Robert returned to the couch, this time sitting nearer to her. "Monika," he said, emphasizing her name, "I know I don't talk much about my situation. The problem is there's—I mean, it's like I'm sitting here in quicksand; and, as crazy as this sounds, it all has something to do with a man—an old man who claims to be—well, actually he hasn't claimed anything at all. Some of my friends here in Wiesbaden claim that he claims to be a mystic of sorts, an alchemist. You know, trying to make gold from lead—that sort of stuff."

"I'm sorry, I don't understand."

"I really don't blame you. All I can say is that he had the strangest affect on me. Everything he says seems—"

"So, you've met this man."

"Twice." There was an awkward pause, and then Robert continued: "As I was saying, everything he says seems to be nonsense, and yet there is something—I promised not see him again."

"Maybe Germany's not so bad, after all. Maybe you like it here."

"Yea, I'm sure you're right," Robert said. "What I mean to say is that, I don't know, I mean we're all on this earth together, right? It's not until we meet each other—meet someone new, a perfect stranger, so to speak—that we're reminded of how similar we all are. I mean, look at us: we're from totally different cultures. Monika, do you also—"

She suddenly kissed him on the lips. Then, with the same suddenness, she pulled back, and looked at him. He was at once confused and excited, and before he could regain his faculties, she stated what was for her an immutable reality: "it must be." Then she repeated it again, this time in German, as if she were declaring it to herself: "*Es muss sein.*" At once there was silence; so completely did she catch Robert off guard. He continued to stare at her, but he no longer talked as he did a few moments before, he did not even smile; he seemed already swept away.

Then he gently pulled her toward him and in a synchronous motion slid his arm around the back of her waist, feeling her skin beneath her sweater. She took part in the action bringing her hand to the back of his neck and running her fingers through his hair. And when he pulled off her sweater—well, the delight at this moment cannot be easily expressed in words. It was like a rush of pure delectation, a feeling of wanting someone to the point of abandon. The only impulse was to be with this person and no other in the world; and there wasn't a moral under the sun that could prevent them from achieving what each so desperately wanted to do.

PART THREE

Citrinitas

Chapter XX

Christmas passed with the ease of any other day. Jürgen and Petra were visiting family in Frankfurt. They had invited Robert to join them, but he declined out of politeness. He could not, however, refuse their invitation for New Year's Eve. They were expecting quite a do—"toasting the king" or such—and Jürgen billed the event as no less than the crown of the year. He was sincerely proud of himself and his party. He declared that there would be no less than eight kinds of mustard on the cold cuts tray; he was willing to stake his reputation on the fact, although Petra had warned him not to talk about it. "Don't talk about it," she said, "Nobody cares about mustard." And she didn't hesitate to remind her boyfriend that he had no reputation. He simply ignored her and hinted at the next meeting at Käfer's being even better after the holidays. Petra, with a caring, but firm look in her eye, reminded Robert of his promise and told him to stay out of trouble.

At the peak of the Michelsberg is an old cemetery. When Robert arrived (it must have taken 20 minutes to cross town) he found it occupied. There were candles speckled across the landscape, on top of gravestones and on the ground, glowing in the dim grayness. Walking along a row of graves, he noticed a group of people leaving a burial. The funeral director had an armful of flowers and was giving one to each mourner. One after the other, each person would approach the hole, drop a flower in, and depart. When the last one had finished, Robert approached the grave, free for the moment of its heavy gravestone. He leaned over the hole which was quite deep. Then he picked up a flower from the ground and dropped it in. It sailed down to the coffin in graceful somersaults.

Monika was also with family today. On the following day, after that sublime night, she called in sick from work. The two spent the entire morning in bed, sipping *Milchkaffee*, reading the paper, and enjoying each other's company beneath the goose-feather comforter. It was one of those wet and windy days when hot drinks and thick blankets were particularly relished. By late afternoon they had decided to take a shower and head down to market for some food. They dined at home by candlelight and a humble bouquet of flowers Robert had picked from the garden in the courtyard. When he left the next day, she kissed him and admitted she would be counting on seeing him after the holidays. Her eyes said even more.

The only way to the top of the Neroberg is via the *Philosophenweg*, or "Philosopher's Way": a path winding through the trees, originally designed to aid spa patients with their cure. From a distance the Neroberg appears as a natural prominence towering over the city like a tsunami frozen before it could break, buttressed by rolling hills of forest that disappear into a dark hinterland. At closer inspection, however, the hill is sliced a hundred times by an elaborate network of serpentine paths leading up to the summit and back into the meadowlands. The Philosopher's Way is the central artery of this system. With hands clasped behind his back, Robert started up the gravelly trail. Looming above was the Russian Chapel, perched at a dramatic standpoint above the city, crowned with its five golden cupolas, and visible as far away as the Rhine. It was built in 1855 as a sepulcher for the mortal remains of the Grand Duchess Elizabeth Michailovna from St. Petersburg, who perished while giving birth to her child.

Upon entering the chapel, Robert was struck with the sight of her effigy, masterfully carved from creamy-white marble, sleeping atop her tomb as if it were merely a brief spell of tiredness that had swept her away and she would reawaken at any moment. The ripples of her pillow had been so expertly crafted that the beholder was at a loss to perceive this was in reality a massive slab of stone. Robert approached her and allowed his finger to lightly glide along the contours of the stonework. It was cool and remarkably smooth to the touch; the carving was delicate and thorough, punctuated by the slightest dips and rises. High above, inside the central tower, stained glass windows threw wisps of blue and pink onto the stone walls; and here, too, there was elaborate gilding and portraiture lining the opening.

Robert turned his head. He was alone except for an attendant tucked behind a wooden counter next to the entrance, displaying postcards, a few plastic crucifixes and some imitation icons. The sizeable man was dressed like a monk in a long black robe, had scraggly hair and a heavy jaw exaggerated by an unkempt beard. It was difficult to tell if he was a real monk or just dressed this way for tourists. Robert smiled, but his gesture was ignored. "What's the matter?" he thought, "Is it a sin to smile? Didn't sell any icons today?" The spooky sentinel just sat there staring.

Then, without a word, the over-sized monk pointed with fully extended forefinger to something near the central nave. It seemed he was indicating vaguely in the direction of an altar bedecked with votive candles and a triptych showing Christ before Pontius Pilate. Robert, confused, approached it and lit one of the candles. As he did, he thought about his friends in the world. The haze of frankincense whirled like the fumes of an oriental pipe, blending with the drone of Gregorian chants. His vision became dim, objects blurred; all was flickering and glowing, echoing and singing, and, as he lost focus, a vivid memory came: an old friend...laughing, the scent of burnt grass...his friend who died in a car accident at the age of 17. The ghostly apparition was elated, laughing uncontrollably, declaring they were the best and nothing could stop them; and yet there was something wrong with its voice. A candle flickered and Robert realized that his friend had had to die.

Chapter XXI

As Robert stepped inside and saw Jürgen waiting for him at the bar, all the tumultuous events of the past week vanished into a fleeting memory. The atmosphere was perfectly unchanged: the oak glowed in the candlelight, the propeller spun idly overhead, the Eiffel Towers beckoned the visitor to join them, and the mass of antiques enshrouded the present with an opiating nostalgia. The bartender, looking a bit tipsy, recognized Robert and nodded as he entered. Standing at the bar with two of the loudest cocktails Robert had ever seen was a pair of golden girls dressed in what must have been their finest gowns. They also nodded as he entered (one nearly losing her dentures in the act). The piano man, who gave a nod, was serving up a saucy version of "Bewitched, Bothered and Bewildered."

People were still dining in the adjacent room. The tables had been decorated with flowers, fresh lavender and daisies, which a few gentlemen had stuck in their buttonholes. At one table was a man with a black frock-coat and a spotted vest; his date was wearing a silk blouse, open to her navel, with lace neck ruffles, topped off by a pink feather boa and artificial eye-lashes. For someone unfamiliar with this place—that is, someone who has never experienced it in person—such descriptions must understandably sound a bit far-fetched; however, at Käfer's, believe it or not, these sorts of costumes were the norm. Robert and Jürgen surely drew more attention in their casual wear than the lady smoking from a violet cigarette extension.

Robert smiled. What looked like another Green Fairy was waiting for him. Jürgen was drinking whiskey, and appeared to be in good humor; but Robert should have paid better attention. It was the first time Jürgen had ordered something without first asking, and his drink was almost empty. A more astute observer would have remarked that he was speaking in a slightly quicker rhythm than usual and a bead of sweat was visible on his brow. Nevertheless, he complimented Robert on his punctuality and reminded him not to be late for his all-important New Year's Eve party.

"I always plan it that way," said Robert, greeting his friend with a firm and sincere pat on the back. "And don't worry about your party; I'm always early, even though this seems to be the only place where you arrive before me. I wonder why?"

Suddenly there came a foreign voice: "The heaviest of words, heaviest of words!" Herr Eberhard appeared without warning, storming into the conversation like a guest of honor late to his own banquet, heralding his entrance by the tapping of his peculiar cane. "A glorious week!" he declared. "Faster than light! And now we're together again! And we'll be together yet again with the same electric rapidity! Luna meets Mercury and the golden One is born! The mere thought of it fills me with joy!"

The man with the pointed beard took Robert's hand in a queer grip (his secret Masonic clutch) in which he folded his fingers and pressed Robert's knuckle with his thumb (Petra was right). He appeared to be in top form this evening, speaking a mile a minute and charming everyone within hearing range. It wasn't until he noticed the dull expression on Robert's face that he realized he was speaking German. Robert didn't know how to react, but greeted him as best he could, commenting rather flatly on his fear of having arrived too late.

"Fiddlesticks!" cried the old man, bumping into the derriere of a corpulent demoiselle at the bar, "The reigns of time are at your fingertips. If you wish to speed it up, repeat events at a quicker rate. If you wish to slow it down, diversify your experiences."

Robert grinned. "Well, if this is true, I'm happy to inform you that I'll be heading back to age fourteen now. Goodbye."

With no regard to the sarcasm, Herr Eberhard raised his arm with a cold imperious gesture of command. "Silence!" he thundered; and as soon as he achieved the desired result (indeed, four other couples stopped talking and turned to see what was happening), he continued, orating in a tone of pure satisfaction: "It's there at the door if you want it. But, mark my words, it won't come to you. Time responds to one thing and one thing only: action! So crack the whip, lad! Make it move!"

Despite the fact that Robert was accustomed to expressing his opinions on virtually every topic and refuting arguments regardless of their stance, this old man left him speechless. It's painfully humbling to come up against a personality stronger than one's own. For in this situation one is stunned and all too often loses charm and degrades into a state of honesty. Robert was no exception. Moreover, the realization that people were eavesdropping only made matters worse; at least five others were now eagerly awaiting Robert's response. "I'm afraid," he said; and then cleared his throat. "I'm afraid you don't know me well, Herr Eberhard. You're talking to a guy who has been very successful at making wrong decisions in life."

With Herr Eberhard there was no argument: only dictation. "Dear lad," he said, "we all do. Mankind can hope to do nothing more. Eve bit the apple and it has been gluttony ever since. And it may not be superfluous to point out here, with due emphasis, that we keep getting better! By Jove, when are we happy making right decisions? You were asking if I profess to be a perfectionist. Well, when you say perfectionist," (Robert recalled nothing of the sort) "you have chosen the apposite epithet for your humble host. For I consider myself a perfectionist in the field of making blunders! If the truth be told, there's nothing more regrettable than sound judgment: creed of the conformist and aspiration of simpletons. The creative soul relishes in the breaking of rules. To measure up takes skill, but to err is an art. It's a nobler endeavor, and at bottom more rewarding." Herr Eberhard opened his wallet and pulled out a card. "Now you see it." He slipped it in Robert's hand. "Now you don't! Listen to me well, my boy; don't read it till I've left. Ah yes, what were we saying?"

"People make mistakes," Jürgen interjected, faithfully trying to help his mentor.

"Bravo, young lawyer! By all means, that's exactly what we were saying! Indeed, of our present company, one of us"—he nodded at Jürgen— "has made it his life's calling to observe the rules and conventions of his folk; or, to put it differently, to measure up. The other one"—now he nodded at Robert—"has chosen to leave behind all that was hitherto normal and predictable to him in the hopes of finding adventure. And as for your humble host,"—he took off his furry cap and pressed it against his chest—"well"—the old man burst into laughter. Robert was staring at him, studying his face, which even at their first meeting he had found startling. It was a strange face, with leathery skin, almost resembling a mask: the whiskers of his beard were thick and bristly; his eyes were heavy and immobile. "As I was saying," he continued, watching Robert in return, "those who break rules are errant, but do not take this assertion in bad faith; because they are also progressive. They will not inherit the earth; they will reinvent it. For it stands to reason that to break one rule is to sire another. The rest of society remains fixed, bearing the laws they believe safeguard their wellbeing. They form the middle-class, which in its mediocrity is unable to revolt but nonetheless preserves the system. But you, my boys, have youth; and thus are equipped with the only possession worth having, the only means of change. The history of the world exists in you and is dependent on you. You are the microcosm that by altering yourselves may alter the universe. But I have spoken out of turn. Forgive me, good fellows; let us tip the glass and converse! Now what were you discussing when I so rudely interrupted you?"

"I've already forgotten," Robert commented, taking a sip from his potent green cocktail. They all chuckled and the subject was dropped, Robert explaining that his drink had made him dizzy. Jürgen, poor Jürgen, who looked as if he had been waiting an eternity for the right moment to break in, excused himself to the washroom, leaving Robert alone with the old man. It was time to test some questions: "Herr Eberhard," he said with boyish curiosity, "have you ever met Jürgen's girlfriend, Petra?"

The old man twitched. It wasn't until Jürgen was out of sight that he came in close to Robert. "You mean Nemesis from the Neroberg?" and then he slapped his young apprentice heartily on the back. "By all means! The advocate of Naturalism; and I don't mean she enjoys trekking around in hiking boots, if that's what you're thinking!" The last pun tickled Herr Eberhard's funny bone even more than the first, and the old man broke out laughing at his own joke. But then he abruptly changed tack, shrugging his shoulders and grumbling to himself; and, as if a judgment had been reached, he angrily snapped: "Doesn't get beyond the organic, that girl: hopelessly factual, tediously empirical—correction: *fatally* empirical. We could fill a book with terms to express her kind, but in the end there's only one: party-pooper!"

"But we all see the world through Nature," Robert pleaded.

"Hogwash. You're sounding more like that harpy by the

minute. To draw an analogy between a sophistic attitude toward the scientific method and the wondrous and well-nigh inscrutable trappings of old Mother Nature is a lamentable piece of intellectual bad taste if ever I encountered one." The old man cleared his throat. "Allow me to put it bluntly: Truth is found in coincidence, not in theory. It's found in the shadows of hunches and intuition, beyond the looking glass and into the rabbit's hole. Verily, if we restricted ourselves to what is sensually perceived, we would end up on an uncomfortably small tip of a gargantuan iceberg."

Then he drew a deep breath. It was clear that this woman perturbed him beyond control, and Robert's interest in her was not received in good humor. He rolled up his sleeves, adjusted his furry cap and scoffed angrily: "It's a case of blatant diligence if ever I saw one. Tragic really, practical to the bone—impelled to call every spade a spade, trapped in her own vicious circle of chicken and egg, not realizing she's laying one every time she opens her snout!"

"What?"

"You heard me. It's a classic case of prissy, pedantic, petty, over-schooling."

"I'm sorry," rejoined Robert, flabbergasted, "but you don't mean to suggest she shouldn't have gone to university, do you?"

The old man laughed without any compunction for offending his present company. "That's exactly what I mean! University? Balderdash! It's the only place I can think of where one develops the spirit at the expense of the soul; the only place where years of free thought are dwindled, chiseled and minimized until there's nothing left but three letters on a dusty sheet of paper! And what's more, for a price! If ever the bourgeoisie concocted a cloaking device for its own inferior pedagogical modus operandi, the ivory tower is it. Didn't you notice the web? That seductively taut veil at the gates of every campus, dangling its thread for the crooked leg of that great bloodsucking spider called skepticism."

"But Herr Eberhard," Robert pleaded, "these words seem contrary to everything you're about!"

"Show me a citizen of Wiesbaden," demanded the old man in a far from discrete volume, "show me just one of these materialistic mediocrities who is not antagonistic to the arts and sciences, not bitten by the *tædium vitæ* of this stagnant spa, not completely out to lunch with this never-ending rest-cure, and I'll prostrate myself before the both of you!"

"But I thought Wiesbaden was a cultural town?"

Herr Eberhard shook his head. "Culture cannot be bought; it must be made. It is for this reason that the rich will always seek the poor for artistic inspiration. Egad, where materialism reigns, conformity blooms and ideas take cover. Do you reckon these burghers have time to think? Boy, there are no artists here, no philosophers, no revolutionaries. These people work for a living! Imagine that! They'll never have the luxury of forgetting the day of the week, never be free of credit, and never know the spiritual benefits of doing nothing."

Robert felt somehow insulted and didn't answer. The old man ignored it; actually, he seemed to be deriving satisfaction from Robert's humbled state. He pushed forward with his oratory as if he had been asked to continue. "The air around here is unpleasant for the creative nose. These bathhouse pools have been still too long; the surface has grown moldy, the bottom has gone to sludge and no one has thought to open a window. Even if you can endure the stench, you won't see an inch beyond the surface. Only when currents flow do we see the depths. The Kurort a cultural town?" and suddenly Herr Eberhard laughed: heartily, but not good-naturedly.

Jürgen returned from the washroom, and, looking ten years younger, tried to rejoin the discussion asking his two colleagues if they had solved the problems of the world while he was gone. Robert couldn't speak. Herr Eberhard, visibly pleased with his young disciple's interest, put his hand on his shoulder as if to physically guide him back into the conversation: "Good Jürgen, good Jürgen," he said stoutly, "we did that years ago! Today we rally for a nobler cause."

"Does this cause have a name?" Jürgen asked.

The old man proudly raised his arm in the air like a general going into battle, tears filling in his baggy bright eyes, and then cried out the word as if to say, "charge!" "Enlightenment!"—The cry thundered true, causing the bartender to bring his finger politely to his lips and two ladies to bashfully giggle—"Tally-ho and take up the gauntlet, men! Transcend these shadows of obscurantism and embrace the cabalistic shine! Grief to those who resist us! It's fisticuffs time!"

"And what shall our weapons be?" Jürgen asked.

"Weapons?" the old man scoffed, his moustache shaking with passion. "The adept need no weapons!"

Robert broke in. "Are you telling us, Herr Eberhard, that you carry no weapons?"

"Neither defensive nor offensive," he asserted. "I was divested of them long ago. My strength lies in my soul and bare hands. I need nothing more. It's marvelous what can be accomplished with these two divine tools. Bear in mind that no tools of iron were used in the building of King Solomon's temple, and no tools of iron will mend the culture that industry has tread upon. Gentlemen, I'm wont to expand on a theme such as this, fascinating as it is, but I hope that for the time being my statements were lucid enough and that my ideas were satisfactory to your youthful thirst for knowledge." And without further ado, Herr Eberhard shook their hands and begged their forgiveness, explaining he must leave immediately; a "colleague" was in urgent need of his assistance. He swiftly made his exit through the same door in the back of the restaurant as the previous week.

"A colleague?" Robert said, perplexed. "Jürgen, you never told me Herr Eberhard has a colleague."

"I know."

"Have you ever met this person?" Robert persisted; attempting to visualize what type would fall into such a category.

"I've not been invited. I don't know anyone who has met him."

"I think I'd like to meet this man."

"So would I," returned Jürgen, swigging down the remains of his drink, "but for the moment I've got another week to eat up. And don't forget the New Year's Eve party. Petra and I have already started with the decorations, and I can tell you it's going to be good this year."

On this note Jürgen paid the bill, shook Robert's hand and left the same way he had entered; that's to say, with a smile. The bar was packed. Four grand dames were now sitting next to Robert, and Jürgen's exit suddenly left him with a feeling of vulnerability. One of the belles caught Jürgen in her sights as he was leaving and let out a pubescent giggle. The other three were spying Robert. The piano player, oblivious to it all, was whipping up a spicy rendition of "New York, New York"; and the same fool as last week was once again playing Mr. Microphone. "But wait," Robert thought—what about the card from Herr Eberhard? Robert took it out of his pocket and examined it. The paper was coarse with a thin gold line bordering it. In the center was written, in bold ebony script, the following: *Repetitio est mater studiorum.* In the lower right corner were the name "Bardo T. Eberhard" and a telephone number. Robert turned the card and found a message handwritten on its backside: "It is high time we met in private. It's regarding the water."

Chapter XXII

The thought had crossed Robert's mind that he was going insane. Not that he was roaming around like a maniac, hysterical or even unconscious of his actions, but he couldn't help seeing connections between the people he was meeting and the water; and this latest bit of evidence, namely the card from Herr Eberhard, was the icing on the cake. There was no way this mention of "the water" could not be referring to the Kochbrunnen. Rationally, he knew this kind of superstition was a bother—worse yet, a hindrance to clear thinking—however, the coincidences seemed to be piling up in droves, and it was becoming more and more difficult to discern meaningful patterns from the normal serendipity of life. And is it not equally naïve to deny everything one cannot explain? After all, even Monika had mentioned the water, and Radovan seemed to have a suspicious affinity to vodka, which is essentially water. It was as if they all knew about his interest in it—indeed, took it for granted—and they were pushing him along this path. And yet this was impossible. Nobody knew how often he was visiting the source.

Robert reached over to the clock and turned it toward him: it was 3:27 in the morning. All of the stress lately—the conflicting advice, recurring guilt and strange coincidences—was clearly affecting his perception of time. The absence of job and responsibility had apparently freed his body of any temporal rhythm: one night he would sleep three hours, the next night he would sleep twelve. Moreover, time itself seemed to be warping under these conditions. Sometimes it flew by with tremendous speed: two or three weeks leaving only trivial souvenirs. Other times it slowed to a halt: six or seven minutes producing everlasting memories.

In essence, his sense of time was anchored in America. In Europe, he lacked the cultural background from which one measures temporal events. For instance, in California he knew that one ought to be driving at 16, voting at 18 and going to bars at 21. In Germany, however, this isn't the case; and accordingly, Robert experienced a loss of temporal responsibility. From his perspective, the clock stopped the minute his plane took off in L.A. four months ago. He imagined his friends were frozen during this time; that they were waiting for him unchanged. Moreover, he believed his own life to have stopped the moment of his departure. If he returned tomorrow, he fancied he would pick up his life right where he had left it off. The experience he was collecting in Germany was somehow exempt from his life back home. It was extra, collected without cost; and if he returned tomorrow, he imagined it would not be withdrawn from his life's temporal account or be visible on his face.

When he woke again it was already after 11:00. In an attempt to assess the weather, he pushed his covers to one side, reached to the window and peeked out over the rooftops of the

Neroberg. There had been a string of snow flurries recently leaving patches of white all over the city. He stuck his head out the small paned window, twisted it a full 180 degrees, and drew a deep, moist breath. The air was fresh and tasted good. He inhaled again, even deeper than the last, and this time counted to thirty before releasing it in a cloud of steam; such was the forecast for the last day of the year.

Robert was glad Jürgen and Petra had invited him to their party. It was to be an intimate fête with no more than six or seven "selected" guests. Beef carpaccio, oysters in the half-shell and lox-on-toast were being served for dinner, not to mention caviar, herring, escargot and a wide array of cheeses. Jürgen was planning to open a favored bottle of champagne for the occasion, and it was guaranteed to celebrate to a bar-full of apéritifs, digestifs, wines and cocktails. He demanded, in his amicably bombastic way, that the soirée be held at his and Petra's place in order to toast Max Weber at midnight. Actually, the way he went on about the toasting, one would think New Year's Eve was invented to help celebrate Weber. It was all Jürgen could talk about during the past weeks. Petra was eager to share her new book on "Rothko and the Dionysian Urge." Monika was still in Weinheim with family.

By the time Robert returned home it was already after four. The light outside was fading and the air was cooling to a nocturnal chill. He collapsed on his bed, staring at the ceiling, heavy in his skin. In the end there's no escape from it. If we spend the day running laps around a track or just stay in bed, after all is said and done, it's the same: both are a form of stagnation and leave one drained. On his nightstand was his wallet. He reached over and took it (there was about ten Euros and the card Herr Eberhard had given him at Käfer's), and then picked up the receiver, dialed the number and waited—no answer. It rang at least seven times. Just as he was about to hang up, the other line was taken, but no one spoke to greet; and after a suspiciously long, static-filled pause, Robert attempted to speak in German: "*Guten Tag, ist Herr Eberhard da, bitte?*"

There was a second pause, and then the old man appeared on the line in a fluster over God knew what, rambling on about how well Robert had done, that is, having followed the aforesaid instructions to a T, and that he was sincerely pleased. Then his voice backed away from the line, mumbling, as though he were consulting someone in the background.

"Herr Eberhard, are you not alone this evening?" Robert said, sensing this was the wrong time to call. "I'm sorry if I'm disturbing you. I can easily call again another time."

"Of course I'm alone!" he hollered, first sounding offended and then segueing into an apology: "Just clearing the throat, you know. It's only this confounded—now Robert, I want you to listen to me. I want your undivided attention. Zeus listens and Athena protects us with the aegis he bequeathed her. Open your heart and confess with the sincerity of the accused." The old man's voice dropped to a whisper: "Are you drinking the water?"

"The water?" Robert asked.

"You know," the former reiterated, employing a devious intonation, as if he were saying something that was risky to both him and to Robert, "*the* water."

"You mean the Kochbrunnen water?"

"Shhh, not too loud."

"Yes, why?"

"Because we don't want *them* to hear."

"I mean why do you care if I'm drinking the water?"

"So you are drinking it!"

"Yes! I just said that!" snapped Robert, his voice trembling with frustration.

Again, there was mumbling in the background, excited deliberation, as if there were two conversations going at once. Herr Eberhard was speaking, but it was difficult to say with whom: "Yes, laudable indeed, but what we—how much, Robert...um...what I mean to say—well, how many times a day do you visit the source?"

"Usually, about four times a day," Robert said. "On a good day five or six." Yet it occurred to him at once that he should not have said this and that by doing so he had admitted Herr Eberhard's right to an interest in his actions; still, that didn't seem important at the moment. His confession brought another pause, followed by more vague discussion, but this time he interrupted it demanding again to know if the old man was alone.

To this, the whispers stopped, Herr Eberhard cleared his

throat, and then thundered through the receiver: "And when will the pedant put down the book!" Robert held the phone away from his ear and then stared at it as if it had come to life. Even at an arm's length the old man's voice could be heard squawking out of the receiver. "What does he want?" Robert thought, and why does he care so much about a little curiosity. Before his absence could be noticed, Robert returned the phone to his ear: "Boy," the old man cried, "at what point are you going to learn to stop questioning everything! On bent knee we beg you, cease with this panophobic fiddle-faddle!"

"You ask too much of me, really. And what do you mean, we?"

"Now Robert, in view of the fact that in principle medicinal springs are curative, this is critically important: have you noticed any change since you've been partaking of the water here in Wiesbaden?"

"What do you mean by the word 'change'?"

"Change in yourself."

"Of course, I've been going through change lately; but you're not going to suggest the water has anything to do with it!"

The mysterious voice still lurked in the background, as though Herr Eberhard, now speaking in the matter-of-fact tone of a family doctor, was doing nothing more than relaying information: "For the moment, double your intake; and never mind what they say about the psychotomimetic side effects. It's pure exaggeration. Yes, double your intake. We'll hold at that for the next couple weeks before making another assessment."

"Psycho what?" Robert pleaded, "Side effects? But I distinctly read on the information panel last week that you shouldn't drink more than a liter a day."

"That's precisely the level we must surpass."

"Are you suggesting the city of Wiesbaden is lying to us?"

"I'm suggesting that if you expect to see results, you need to drink more. The superbly rich mineral content has a real affect. You must have noticed this; and seen from this standpoint, I believe you can grasp that it's only through volume that you may achieve real change. Admittedly, all the hullabaloo around the magical qualities of this water gives my request an air of nonsense on account of which it may be deservedly objectionable to your ears. All the same, we should beware of emptying out the baby with the bath water. At the core of this myth is a valid healing effect."

"Okay, Herr Eberhard."

"Well, do you agree or not?"

"Sure, I agree," Robert said; and so cornered, he felt that he did agree, but there was something in him that recoiled from such a brash command.

"It is also highly recommended that you save a certain portion of the liquid for the treatment of your follicles—does wonders, you know—massage it in, counter-clockwise strokes only! Highly advisable, yes; you'll sprout the ebony locks of Samson himself!"

146

"This is totally ridiculous!" Robert blurted out, far too aggressively. The frustration was seething up in him, and he was unable to control it; he thought that this cheeky old man didn't know where to stop; the conversation had gone too far and it was time to hang up. Really, it was as if Robert was nothing more than the brunt of his practical jokes.

"Heed what I say, boy; it's of the utmost importance that you do not go out tonight."

"What?"

"You heard me; don't go out."

Robert burst into nervous laughter. "I'm sorry Herr Eberhard, but that's impossible. It's New Year's Eve, for Christ's sake! And Jürgen and Petra have invited me to a special dinner party—they've been going on about it for months—and I simply can't say no. I won't say no."

"My boy," said the old man in that uniquely authoritative tone that nature bestows upon fathers when it's time to put their little tikes in place, "think about the unit of a second, the speed of a minute, the distance of an hour. Now, I beg you, think about five thousand years—and not as a mass of time, but as a single great unit; one massive step in history. Look up; the comet that hailed the Messiah twenty centuries ago has returned—and perhaps the devout are right; perhaps their savior is coming again in some unknown barn or this time in an apartment in the city. How can we know for sure? Years will pass before he or she is ripe to display this congenital divinity. Regardless of what is to unfold, due to the numbers alone it will have a tremendous historical impact. And that energy will affect everyone; I promise you this! Wars will be ignited and extinguished under the historical pressure to make something happen when the clock strikes zero. For it all will be remembered. Yes, just as when an earthquake strikes, or a monarch is felled, the shock of the historical impact causes the memory to retain the moment in vivid detail for the remainder of its life. And this is the historical environment we're in. It will all be retained! In vivid detail—and not merely within the mind of humanity, but within the consciousness of history. For cardinal events aren't easily forgotten, and just as Christ lived during that exquisite instant when history recalled his every move, the pen will cherish the decades to come. I guarantee it with the conviction of the enlightened. And you'll be alive to see it! Boy, I implore you, don't go out tonight. Stay in your room. Bolt the door. Focus on the future and dare not dilute it with the banality of the present. Join the adept, and concentrate your faculties on what is happening within; deem it within the context of history as a whole, not these years that pass undetected. Look deep into your heart and find the foresight to live beyond the moment. Understand yourself! Understand life! And, above all, drink the water!'

Robert couldn't answer: for all that this man had to offer, choice was not on the list. There were no ifs, ands, or buts, no question marks, and no appeals. Indeed, it was the first time he had ever met someone who so completely and resolutely denied him this basic right. It was disconcerting, and it was exhilarating. There was talking again in the background, but this time Robert didn't question it: "Herr Eberhard, it's strange what you ask of me."

"You must, my son."

"But what should I say to Jürgen and Petra?"

"I'm sure you'll think of something."

"But why?"

"Don't ask why," he said roughly and then changed his tone. "You may not realize it, my child, but as we speak you're blossoming from a heathen into a neophyte."

"I honestly don't understand a word you say."

"Go now!" commanded the old man with his punctuated manner of speech—"go *now*! Find the sea and drink from the Water of Life! We've much to discuss in the following days. Carry out my orders and await the results. Your trust in me has been acknowledged from the beginning and, as I communicated to you at the regular meeting place, I believe it's time we meet in private. I have someone I'd like you to meet, though from the outset I'll warn you this is a person unlike any other you've encountered. I shall call you tonight, as the clock strikes twelve, and instruct you as to where the rendezvous will take place. I hope you appreciate the confidence I'm showing you; and, I should hasten to add, it goes without saying that this little parley shall be repeated to no one. This is our secret. Is that clear?"

Disturbed to the core by this request that, as implying a need for secrecy, seemed unaccountably strange to him, there was nothing for Robert to do but comply. "Herr Eberhard," he pleaded once more, "who's there with you? I can hear two of you speaking."

"I must leave you now. Do as I ask, and we'll speak again soon"—and before Robert could get a word in edgewise, the old man hung up.

Chapter XXIII

It is not advisable to feel kinship with an obvious lunatic, nor did Robert do so. And yet all the next day he couldn't get Herr Eberhard out of his head. He was distraught and forgetful; he couldn't concentrate on his chores, and, to catch up on his homework, he had to stay in the library two hours longer than usual. Now it may well be that the conversation was longer than he recalled, but what remained in memory illustrated at least the nature of Herr Eberhard's preoccupations and added a stroke or two to Robert's sketchy picture of him—and the picture wasn't pretty. It seemed that every obligation was coerced from Robert by dint of persuasion and guile without the slightest indication of benevolence. Under such circumstances it is small wonder that Robert didn't hang up, or at least refuse the unreasonable demand, but everything was over before he had a chance to process it. The exchange had left him completely bewildered, at moments frustrated, and yet more than ever, he wanted to get to know this man.

Passing the Kochbrunnen on his way home he couldn't resist stopping to watch a few retirees gathered around the fountain; but when he did, they froze and turned to see what he was doing, unanimously glaring at him as though he had done something wrong. Without acknowledging their curiosity he moved on toward the Taunusstrasse, and it was in this jumbled state of mind that he returned to his attic, panting from his hike up the hill, to find a letter on his bed.

He knew from whom it was. Merely the presence of this envelope, heedfully placed on the pillow, its familiar cursive script and colorful stamp, foretold a bracing and well-needed confrontation with his past. Sybille hadn't forgotten him. Nevertheless—perhaps from fear, perhaps from neglect—four days passed before he opened it.

Berkeley, December 23rd

Dear Robert,

Until now, I've not had the strength to write you. How could you have left me the way you did, without calling or writing? Never has a man treated me with such disrespect. I desperately needed to hear from you, but you weren't there. Weeks went by like this. And then the weeks became months. How could you neglect me the way you did, if you truly loved me? Was it a lie what you said? I could never have left you in such a way. I needed your love, and yet you left me without a reason. We were supposed to live together. I'm sure you could have found work here through one of your friends. Have you forgotten every promise you made?

You said you would write me every day. I can remember you saying that your interest in learning German was an interest in me. Your "short" trip to Germany was supposed to be an attempt to get closer to me, to understand me. If this was true, then how come you never wrote? And knowing full well that I came to America for you! That was the first time I had made such a commitment to a man. You violated it. I will never understand that. My eyes fill with tears as I think of it. And you knew I had no friends here. You knew I was alone.

As I sit here at my desk, more than four months after you left, all I have from you is this postcard written the week you got there. And I'm sorry, but it's incredible what you wrote. Every word reveals an egocentrism completely lacking any concern for me. Not once did you speak of seeing me. You simply begged for me to write like we were still together! Are you crazy? As far as I'm concerned, we broke up three months ago!

I [crossed out and re-written again] *I won't go into details, but my life has moved on. For the moment I'm hopeful, and only through the support of a special person, I'm beginning to let go of the anger that has filled me during the past months. I can see now that I've been lucky. And I will do my best to learn from the mistakes I've made with you. I wish you luck, Robert, and I hope you find whatever it is that you're looking for. Don't write back.*

Goodbye.
Sibylle

Robert read the letter once, neatly folded it back up and returned it to its envelope. He slowly let his body recline onto the bed until he was lying flat on his back, fully dressed. Her English skills were definitely improving, he thought, gazing at the envelope on the nightstand; her style, however—considering the touchiness of the matter—was somewhat direct. There was a certain phrase there: "I will do my best to learn from the mistakes I've made with you," which put it all too clearly, and there was also the suggestion that Robert was the sole cause of this situation, getting his just desserts. Her remark was insulting, though perhaps unintentional. She had obviously grown up in a scientific household (she probably didn't believe in Santa Claus or God) and her newfound language skills made not the slightest change towards a more literary sensibility for metaphor in lieu of the straightforward. Be that as it may, her efforts were noble. The drafting of such letters is no easy task; the blood boils as we see our ugly reality taking form and permanence on the page, and we inevitably overwrite, revealing emotions that would be better left in the shadows of our souls. Indeed, considering the linguistic obstacles, it was an admirable attempt at communication: nothing to publish, but an admirable attempt just the same.

Now Robert remembered that, in fact, he had told all this to Sybille the last time he saw her; but notwithstanding the logic she was made of, on that occasion she broke down and cried like a child. It was right after his decision to leave for Germany, and she had attempted in a similar manner—via a letter (though at the time there was no need to post it)—to express her feelings of dissent toward the situation, which, when all was said and done, came across with the clumsiness of a dog. Robert was suddenly appalled by these thoughts; firstly, that they passed through his mind at such an inappropriate moment; and, secondly, that they had disappeared for months and then reappeared as if of their own accord, like tiny buzzing mosquitoes that distract one from a relevant subject. Needless to say, Sibylle was the most significant woman in his life. What's more, she was a good person. The pain he caused her must have been considerable, and he surely inflicted irreparable emotional damage. He visualized her crying; imagined nights spent alone; saw her walking home in the dark, afraid of what lurked in parked cars, realizing nobody cared; then came the shamelessly precise imaginings of Sibylle giving herself to another man, enjoying it, and, worse yet, that she could fall in love with him, that this stranger could become the light of her life. Ultimately, Robert attempted to take on the pain he had dealt out. He tried as hard as he could, and yet he felt nothing.

Robert was aware he had undergone an inexplicable change

during the past months, and yet this queer tinge of apathy caught him off guard. But it was not an unpleasant feeling; quite the contrary, he had the impression he had just scored a victory and someone invisible was applauding him for it. His intellectual capacities were clear. In fact, they were stronger than ever. He could critically view himself and his situation with a clarity of thought that would impress most therapists. And yet he felt nothing in his heart, no pain, no regret. On the contrary, he felt a degree of relief that he would no longer be plagued by his moralistic memories of the neglected girlfriend. A level of maturity had just been reached where he no longer felt impelled to pour salt on the wounds of love. Ten years ago, he would have done anything to get Sibylle back, absolutely anything; all for the chance to prolong the relationship another couple of hopeless months, precisely long enough to dump the poor woman rather than being left himself.

He now found himself above all that. She asked him to not write back, and for once he was about to respect that wish. He could read into the letter that she still loved him. She gave him what she could, and at this point in his life it was simply not enough. In turn, he also failed to meet her needs, causing her to do what any level-headed person would do: find a new mate. All this shot through Robert's mind as he reached beside his bed and took one of the bottles he had fetched last night on his walk.

Then at once the intoxication gave way to anguish: there had to be an end to this. Sooner or later he would have to put an end to these betrayals! Sooner or later he would have to commit to something! He thought of Monika, and then of Petra, adding guilt to this odious concoction. He had enjoyed his time with them as if Sibylle were sitting by his side. She wasn't. She was probably alone, crying herself to sleep and finding the strength to rebuild her life on her own. All his spleen rose up within him and he was overcome with revulsion, for himself and everything around him—it was exaggerated and inappropriate—as if the guilt of his entire life had finally caught up with him and this episode was merely the catalyst for a flood of regrets. For the truth had reared its ugly head: he was only capable of living from his own needs. And what a task this was! To feed that insatiable beast that was his own self-love.

There was no doubt about it, his emotions were in a flux; but then, thank God, the melancholy passed. Surely things weren't as bad as they seemed. Indeed, the burden that had mercilessly racked him just moments before was now on the retreat. Sound and steady logic was reclaiming its rightful place. At a certain level, he thought, unscrewing the bottle and taking a good, long swig, it was egocentric to believe she was so deeply affected by him to begin with. The more he thought about it, the better he felt. Sibylle was able to conceptualize her emotions well, leaving him free of any little mysteries to bother him when he was alone. His slate was wiped clean; and he could now devote even more energy to Herr Eberhard and the yet-to-be-fully-understood water. He took another sip. The only way to avoid the pain of life is by living it. Action is the solvent. It's quite simple if one thinks about it.

Robert let the sacred draft swirl around his mouth with the savor of a wine taster. The flavor was completely different once it had cooled down. It tasted like pure stone.

Chapter XXIV

It was difficult explaining to Jürgen and Petra that he couldn't make it to their party. Indeed, they were shocked when he told them his grandfather had fallen ill and he felt obliged to stay home lest someone call bearing somber news. Jürgen offered his phone of course, and was willing to cover the cost if Robert wished to call his relatives. It was a touching display of friendship; touching, but ineffective. As a final effort to re-win Robert, Petra broke in and pleaded to his good judgment that he should join them, warning that he was going against his instincts by doing it. After all, just as the sick grandfather had a need for companionship, so did Robert. To stay alone at such a time made no sense at all. Her voice trembled with frustration, but politeness kept her appropriate. In the end they both conceded. Whatever it was that weighed on Robert's heart, it was serious enough that he refused to budge with his unexpected decision.

And as the unwritten laws of friendship dictate, one's word must be enough. Neither Jürgen nor Petra pushed the subject beyond the bounds of respect.

Just as the letter from Sibylle presented Robert with a feeling of freedom, so did the little white lie he told Jürgen and Petra. The moment he hung up, he was filled with a rush of satisfaction: Nature's gift to the eudemonist. He had won the gift of time, and was rewarded for his fib with a splendid afternoon. He felt himself clever; smiling to all of society's best as he proudly marched down the Taunusstrasse. And when he arrived at the Kochbrunnen, he came prepared with no less than six empty bottles. It was a special day, indeed. It was the day he doubled his intake. From this moment onward, his life became an experiment acted out upon itself: a vainglorious project with a burning, omniscient light at the end of the tunnel. And thus like the curious Dr. Jekyll who drank from his own phial, driven by the desire to know himself better, Robert chose to obey Herr Eberhard and the mysterious voice in the background. He was eager to see the results because he knew whatever should appear would ultimately be a reflection of his self. For it is only during these moments of intense disorientation that we can claim to be truly living. Unmoored from our anchorage, we drift into a deepening sea, aware from the onset of the dangers lying on that path, half-courting those dangers, in fact, while feigning to deny them. The knowledge of this brings about the purest delight: the feeling of living oblivious to what the morrow will yield, and, as

Petra would argue, this is our most natural state of being.

The unpredictability, which had come to be the rule rather than the exception during the past weeks, by no means was helping Robert with the crisis that had brought him to Wiesbaden to begin with. It was, however, providing him with a source of happiness; and for this he appreciated the strange occurrences that were now presenting themselves on a daily basis. He embraced the peculiar direction his life was taking, this new and untrodden course, inviting his experiences to escort him to the brink, if that was their wish. And he promised himself to be open and, as best he could, not to question why. It's true, there's an entirely unexplored universe of knowledge to be acquired without this cumbersome word.

Chapter XXV

On the night of Saint Sylvester—that is, New Year's Eve— the telephone did ring at precisely midnight. It nearly went unnoticed under the flood of church bells, honking horns, cries of joy and fireworks of all shapes and sizes. From his window Robert watched the dazzling flashes in the moonless sky, the brilliant coruscation and burning sulfur that from a distance looks beautiful. At length he grabbed the receiver, but before he could open his mouth, Herr Eberhard was off and running.

"Boy!" he cried, "We bathe in sublimity! The bells chime with a euphonious cadence unique to this moment! Can you feel it? The god Thoth is visiting us now! And by the gifts of technology, you're able to experience it with us. Listen, can you hear it?"

In the background a strange chanting could be heard. At first notice one would take it for Gregorian. The language, however, was tonally more foreign and the sounds from which the words sprung were almost inhuman. At moments it was as if an animal were present. Robert didn't know how to react: "Herr Eberhard, what's going on over there?"

"It is only I and the thrice majestic Thoth, inventor of signs and guardian of the quill, white ape and brother of those who cherish the moon, who has come all the way from distant Hermopolis along the shores of the Nile."

"Well, the two of you are making quite a ruckus!"

"The baboon! The baboon!" wailed the old man, and then a large crash followed by an unearthly howl could be heard on his end of the line. "Oh, you should be here to witness this event! The dervish whirls! Atman breathes! We effect the sacred knot! Egad, Thoth is magnificent! My boy, the sooner you join our little mystery, the better. The fact you awaited our call was a step in the right direction. We had no doubt you'd remain faithful to us."

Something about the old man's stalwart conviction produced

a uniquely disquieting feeling, almost offensive. Robert considered telling him he had to go, but then said: "Sometimes I suspect you know me better than myself, Herr Eberhard."

"By Zeus," he declared, "of course I do! How can I not, considering I *am* you?" Robert fell silent. "I am you," repeated the old man, his voice dropping to a whisper. "Who else did you think I was? It's fantastic, boy. Through some twist of fate, a clot in the hourglass or a ripple in time, you're getting the chance to gaze upon the portrait of your own golden age. Meeting me is meeting your future."

Robert listened suspiciously; he liked neither this man's feverish pitch nor the bizarre predictions. "That's funny, " he said, "I didn't know I had one."

"Can't you see it, lad? Everyone you're meeting is merely a reflection of yourself."

"That's a nice thought," Robert rejoined, "but you forget my coming here hasn't been much more than a mistake."

"There are no mistakes!" the old man yelled. "It's a teleological fact. Your destiny has been determined since the beginning. I could sense it the moment I met you at the source. And with the proper tools that destiny can be accessed, seen like the luster in a crystal ball! You ought to consider yourself lucky. Do you realize that not everyone in this world has a destiny? From the moment their infant flesh meets the chill air, most are nudged by the stumpy hand of banality. But you Robert, you've been caressed by the gods, and your soul bears the mark of destiny. You will not follow the life of the average. You will be channeled into the path of the adept. Admittedly, you find yourself amidst a difficult passage, what appears to be an insuperable obstacle: a labyrinthine path leading you to the grave, the natural vessel, into the darkness of the solar eclipse; but this is exactly what you need! How else can the Phoenix take flight? The secret is that only that which can destroy itself is truly alive; and your destiny is your life. It pulses through your veins with life-giving force for it is the purest truth. This is what we call *our* truth: the truth of the blood; and to deny this primal force is to embrace confusion. Abandoning the truths of the blood begets restlessness, restlessness begets meaninglessness, and the lack of meaning in life is a soul-sickness whose full import our age has yet to comprehend."

Robert's head was reeling; and yet something in him responded strongly to this deceitful game of cat and mouse. He craved these words like bread to a starving soul, absorbing every thought like air into lungs. It was at once calming and alarming, quickening his pulse as if these poisonous ideas were flowing through his tissue and muscle before reaching his mind. He found it difficult to speak: "I'll admit, I'd like to think this all true; but my own predictions are less optimistic."

"Of course they are," the old man reassured, "We'd expect nothing more from you. But don't forget these old bones bear the wisdom of time. Our view is different. Learn to live from your deathbed, boy. Don't see life from the present looking into the future. See it from the future looking back into the present. We can see your future because we're in it. And the message we send back is 'don't worry'. We have faith in you."

Another cry could be heard in the background, followed by three loud bangs, a howl, and then more chanting. Robert was perplexed. There was no way in heaven this old man was going to convince him a deity had simply popped in to help celebrate the new year and was now smashing the place to bits. If Herr Eberhard was up to some gag, or worse yet lying for the sake of trickery, Robert was going to get to the bottom of it: "What the heck is all that noise, Herr Eberhard? Can you please tell me what you're doing?"

"I, my respectable comrade, am doing nothing," he calmly declared to the tune of a glass exploding against a wall. "It is the god Thoth reorganizing his surroundings. He has promised to transmute into Hermes Trismegistus before the night is through, and if the white ape should be successful, it will be of paramount importance. He has been attempting it for years."

Robert was at the end of his rope. He pleaded to the old man to "speak English for God's sake," and told him that he would be happy if he could understand a fraction of what was being said.

The elder reassured his younger counterpart: "It's only a matter of time. All we ask is that you do as we ask. We shall meet as planned in my personal exedra exactly seventy-two hours from now, and we will be three. Yes, seventy-two hours from this moment, from this second. That is to say, seven minutes past the zero hour on Friday: day of women, dedicated to Freya, known as Venus in the lands west of the Rhine, in January: month of Janus, protector of doors and gateways, and hence of beginnings—verily, an excellent day to meet!"

"And what, if I may ask, is your 'personal exedra'?"

"It's my discussion room, of course. What is a domicile without a library, a study and an exedra? Don't you agree?"

"Of course. And how might I find you, Herr Eberhard?"

"By locating Parkstrasse 3," he proclaimed, as if referring to a ship. "The easiest way to access it is via the Kurpark. You'll notice a gateway near the bust of the Kurdirektor. Approach it, rub the head of the owl and then ring the bell to your left three times before passing. It is of vital importance that you obey these instructions. Once in the garden you will see the house in which my residence is located. Entry can be made by way of the red door. You will see my name. Stand square to the door, knock once, wait, and then knock twice more. We shall instruct you from there."

Robert propped the phone on his shoulder and scribbled the instructions on a torn piece of paper. "I've just noticed it's become calm on your end of the line. What happened?"

"Thoth is meditating, presumably in a state of trance, level six according to our system of measurement. He needs all the energy he can muster up if he hopes to successfully undergo the transmutation. This is not something one does everyday, you know. And believe me, your turn will come. What is remarkable is the way in which he is able to keep his body erect while suspended between those two chairs. The strength needed to avoid falling must be considerable, and yet he appears to be totally relaxed. If all goes well, the transmutation should occur within the next four hours."

"The next four hours? Don't you ever sleep?"

"Robert, listen to me," the old man pleaded, his voice becoming strangely desperate. "Before I go, I have a question to ask. Tell me in earnest; were you ever in the Russian chapel atop the Neroberg?"

"Yes, last week on Christmas day. Why?"

"Now lad, be honest with me, did you visit the sarcophagus: the one that entombs the ill-fated princess? And did you light a candle?"

"Why yes, I did."

"Did you light a second candle?"

"How did you know that?"

"And, at the moment you lit the second candle; did you think of someone who died? Someone close to you. Someone young like the princess. Think about him again, my boy. Think about your friend one more time; before you sleep tonight."

"But—I don't want to."

"Let him come to you, and listen. It's the words of Death that come in your sleep. It's necromancy."

"It was long ago."

"Listen to your friend."

"I want to forget."

Chapter XXVI

It was a moonless night, and the dome was lit from inside, strangely illuminating the steam from the fountain, which danced and twirled in the air, reaching into the blackness like bony fingers. It was difficult to grasp the antiquity of this spot, and to imagine who else had partaken from this source whose fluid rose from the abyss of time immemorial. Robert took his cup from his backpack, filled it, and diligently brought the steaming water to his lips. The air was cold, and the piping ebullition tasted exquisite as it entered his mouth, trickling down his throat with the anodyne caress of opium, soaking deeply into his chest, boiling within him. It felt as though it had collected in his lower back, warming his kidneys and enkindling his spine. He felt penetrated by it, possessed by it, as if it were nursing and suffocating him at once. A few minutes passed in this way before he started again for Käfer's.

As he entered, a hostess appeared to help him with his coat. In the corner was a trio of golden girls, and near the back entrance, accompanied by a half-empty bottle of wine was a woman smoking a cigarette and staring off into space. After Robert had taken his place next to Jürgen at the bar, she shifted her chair, in order to sit with her back to them. Jürgen explained in a low voice that she was a regular customer and one shouldn't take it personally.

"I'm sorry I missed your party, Jürgen."

"Don't worry about it," he said, jabbing his spectacles back on his nose; and then he squinted at Robert, as if something were on his mind. "How's your grandfather?"

Robert replied hesitantly, trying to avoid the subject he had opened. The bartender placed his drink down, and then a pause ensued, as Robert was unable to look his friend in the eye. Near the piano was a couple peering into each other's eyes, silent, as if in the grips of a psychic tête-à-tête. They were sitting at a window table, facing each other against the cream colored curtain, their faces lighted by a red-shaded table lamp.

Jürgen asked what Robert was thinking to which he quickly came up with a lie about a movie he had recently seen about a sick old man. It was supposedly about a boy in London who had to nurse his dying grandfather all alone. But with every bit of small talk the shame was building, for this silly escapade and mediocre fib were at Jürgen's expense. In the end Robert couldn't bear it, and confessed: "Forgive me Jürgen, I lied to you and Petra last night."

"It doesn't matter," he returned, unaffected.

"I stayed home to receive a call from Herr Eberhard."

Jürgen smiled. "Don't ever think you need to be honest with me, Robert. Our friendship is stronger than that."

Robert was touched, and in a moment of reckless sincerity decided to share for the first time his strange interest: "Jürgen, do you ever drink the water from the Kochbrunnen?"

"Of course, we all do."

Robert looked at Jürgen with almost panic in his eyes.

"Even Petra, although she admits it to no one. They say it keeps you young, but I haven't seen the results."

Robert tried to regain his composure. "It's apparently healthy."

"It's apparently toxic!" corrected Jürgen, rattling the ice in his glass. "According to Petra, any more than a liter per day and your body will be saturated with lithium."

"I really don't know who to believe anymore."

Jürgen shook his head disparagingly. "But Robert," he said, "must you always put such importance on truth? You act as if a little lie here and there is going to destroy the universe! Don't worry so much. There's nothing wrong with telling lies. Everyone does it—some of us more than others—although most people forget it's a harmless activity, because it always leads to truth. What's offensive is the way people carry their so-called honesty around like a big piece of garlic, expecting it to chase away all the evils in the world." He put his hand on Robert's shoulder and pointed to the corner. "Now look at these three women. They believe they'll meet a man tonight. They believe they're in the big city. They believe they're living the luxury life. It's thanks to them that we can enjoy this special atmosphere. If Käfer's ever let truth cross its door, the place would be out of business within a week! And what is so great is that the moment some middle-aged, balding, overweight man comes in with the same dream, the fantasy magically becomes reality. Are you going to be the one to tell them this isn't Paris? Not I."

"I'm glad I met you, Jürgen."

"The next round, I buy," he declared with a grin. "Let's drink to Wiesbaden and all of its lies!" He could see he was lifting Robert's spirits. "My god, imagine Sophia Loren off-screen? Why, she'd be mortal! We never fall in love with truth. It can be our friend, but never our lover. It's always fantasy who takes us in her arms." He took another sip and smacked his lips. "And that's the way it should be! Without it there can be no love: only cold reproduction. It's through idealism that we inspire our partners to romance. And if the ideal is a lie, then let me live in ignorance! Is it not ignorance we share? Truth we find alone; a lie takes two."

Jürgen's thought had a curious logic. Indeed, in light of this mounting delirium it seemed normal. After all, if Robert ventured to share a mere fraction of the far-fetched episodes of late, the world would label him a liar. If he told the truth, he would be banished from normal society. He would be alone.

The two young men relaxed some moments, following the gentle swishes of the propeller overhead. Robert raised his glass, took a sip of the potent jade nectar, and then gazed across the bar. The woman near the back entrance had sunk even deeper into her melancholy. Although she was clearly mature in years, her hands were smooth and youthful; she had limber fingers and well-manicured nails long enough to attract attention, on the verge of curling, and painted with a thick and glossy coat of blood red varnish. She was garbed in formal attire, although there was no opera tonight. Without moving his eyes, Robert asked if Herr Eberhard had been in.

"No, not at all," Jürgen answered, sipping his whiskey.

Robert nodded despondently. "How come he always arrives through the back door instead of the front?"

"Some believe he lives in the Kurhaus," Jürgen explained, looking over his glasses and making a ghoulish face. "He's never seen at normal hours, and it's always in this part of town he's found. Sometimes he appears at the opera, in the shadows of one of the boxes, or late at night in the Kurpark, speaking to himself in Latin. Once he was seen at the Kaiser Friedrich Bad with the Kurdirektor, and it's said he steals large amounts of water from the Kochbrunnen in the little hours of the morning."

"He is an eccentric one, isn't he," commented Robert.

Jürgen agreed: "It takes a special type to wear a Russian hat backwards." Robert wanted to tell his friend that he had been invited to the old man's house, but refrained. Deep in his heart he felt that he should share this news; and yet something in him shrank at explaining why he was chosen over his friend, and thus imparted with a responsibility to the old man as well, albeit one for which he never asked. For all of Jürgen's theory on truth and lying, the practice was no less difficult. In the end, Robert guided the conversation away from what was really at hand.

"And you know nothing of his 'colleague,' as he puts it?"

"Nothing," Jürgen replied straightly. "No one has ever seen this person in the flesh."

"Mysterious."

"Some say his colleague doesn't exist at all. Petra is convinced Herr Eberhard has a 'multiple personality disorder'." (He had problems saying this in English) "On top of that, she says he's schizophrenic."

"Schizophrenic?" Robert protested. "Split personality? Now that's going a bit far, don't you think?"

Not in Petra's opinion: "She read a book on the subject to make her point," Jürgen explained. "Supposedly, not all schizophrenics go directly to the sick house. The truth is many are charming. They often have a quick sense of humor, but suffer from paranoia. In extreme cases, they feel surrounded by a hostile world, and fight this fear with delusions and multiple personalities."

"But how can they remain functional?"

"Surprisingly, many do," answered Jürgen, toasting his friend with a fresh whiskey. "If they're rich, they can survive quite well."

"I just can't buy that."

"And why not?" the young lawyer asked, insulted. "Do you mean to tell me everyone here is normal?"

"More or less," conceded Robert.

"Exactly," Jürgen said in an odd tone of voice; he was on the verge of adding something, but, glancing at the barkeeper, who was now looking fixedly at him, too, changed his mind. They suddenly fell silent. There was something strange about it.

For the remaining moments not much was said. The barkeeper was now chatting with a waitress near the door to the kitchen, looking at his watch and motioning for her to leave. The woman near the back entrance hadn't budged. Her lonely eyes, blackened with mascara, continued to stare with a distinctly hopeless expression. One couldn't help wondering what stories she held; that she had nobody to support her; that she was forced to fend for herself; that, perhaps, having been abandoned or widowed, she had chosen this evening as a last ditch effort at love, only to be stood up again. Her cigarette had almost burned itself out; ashes were on the table. The fumes twirled into the air, mixing with her solemn gaze, losing themselves amidst the antiques. She had ever so subtly brought her lip under her teeth. She was beautiful.

Chapter XXVII

At long last, after what had seemed an eternity, Robert made up his mind to cancel his meeting with Herr Eberhard. This was no light matter; and the decision did not come without a considerable expenditure of energy on his part. The predicament played itself out like a game of chess. With arms crossed behind his head, Robert lay in his bed in a cold sweat, probing each plan of attack at least four moves down the line in hopes of catching a mental glimpse of the outcome. He considered the old man's feelings and the repercussions of refusing an invitation from someone whom possessed a uniquely inflated ego and stalwart pride. Granted, when it concerned himself, Herr Eberhard showed no particular interest in punctuality or appointments (the meetings at Käfer's was a perfect example of this), but the fact remained that Robert had given his word. And what about Jürgen? Would this not be pitting the two against one another? An act of favoritism on Robert's part could jeopardize his friend's standing with the old man. It all appeared to be a stalemate. And yet Robert's conviction prevailed. There was something wrong about Herr Eberhard giving him special treatment when Jürgen had clearly invested more in the friendship.

But during the next days Robert found it impossible to exchange even a word with Herr Eberhard. He tried to get a hold of him by every means he could think of, but the old man managed to elude him. On Thursday, after Käfer's, he went straight to the Kochbrunnen and sat down on a nearby bench, watching the steaming fountain and hoping the old man would appear. But the old man didn't turn up, and after a while, it was difficult to say how long, he went home and with no concern for the time phoned Herr Eberhard. He wanted to share his decision, to tell him that the meeting was off, nicely of course, as not to belittle his generous offer, but nonetheless to let him know that a private meeting without Jürgen wasn't needed. But the old man couldn't be reached—not that evening and not the following day.

Hence, unwilling to give up, Robert decided to write a formal letter of refusal; surely fitting to someone with old-fashioned values. As he took to drafting the letter, however, he found it impossible to make his point without revealing his mistrust. Seeing his thoughts on paper was disconcerting; the permanence of the script exaggerated the ideas, transforming them into glaring confessions of discontent. Moreover, by sending this statement of rejection via the post, Robert would be relinquishing the chance to defend his good intentions; once it was sent, there would be no turning back. In the end, he tore up the letter and discarded it. He promptly returned to the telephone and with renewed force made every effort to reach the old man at home. The phone rang indefinitely, late at night and early in the morning, midday and afternoon, and after a while Robert gave in to the idea that it would be easier to go than to stand him up and renege on a promise.

Chapter XXVIII

Thus Robert kept his promise; and, with unexpected anxiousness, here he was, moments after jumping a fence, alone in the Kurpark on one of the gloomiest nights he had ever seen. At least he had been punctual; midnight was striking as he brushed off his pants and started into the park. The gate was surely located where Herr Eberhard described it. The problem was one couldn't see a thing in this murky brume. It was a night from another era; not a night of baneful monsters and demonic cries, nor was it a night of insidious mischief, of sneaking about and ill-doing. It was rather a night of blackest black, when shadows coalesce into a strangling knot and stifle the intruder with a primordial darkness.

It wasn't until Robert had stumbled around the lake three times before noticing the statue to the side of the path near a patch of oaks. He thought the house would be recognizable by a sign his imagination had left unspecified or by some unusual form looming out of the night, but Parkstrasse, where the house was said to be and whose name suggested a proximity to the park, was nowhere to be seen. Could Herr Eberhard have made a mistake about the location? How could anyone be sure with such a man? Robert went back to the main entrance, waited undecidedly for a while, and then circled around the lake once again to make sure that the house wasn't hidden behind a wall or bushes. It was an interesting occurrence: from the path, the bust of the Kurdirektor appeared to be alone. When one arrived at it, however, a trail appeared into the trees.

But no gate was to be seen; and Robert was becoming annoyed that he had not been given better directions. Herr Eberhard showed a strange laxity in his treatment of Robert, and, if he could ever find the house, Robert intended to tell him. Then he caught sight of something ahead. It appeared to be a gate. Even in the darkness, one could see it was in a state of decay. Atop the right column was a stone sculpture of an owl. Robert struck a match to have a better look and the moment the flame ignited, the glaring red eyes of the bird jumped out, startling our hero, the trespasser. He held up the match for a closer look. Someone had ground out its eyes and replaced them with rhinestones. Beneath it, attached to the column, was a bell. As per order, he rung it three times, though the sound didn't travel far through the trees; and it wasn't likely anyone could hear it.

Counting each step, Robert made his way through the damp bush. It was evident the garden hadn't been tended to in years; shrub and weed wildly overgrown in all directions, neglected mounds of dirt, dead branches all around. He paused for a moment and tried to focus on the house he was attempting to reach, which now stood before him as an imposing gray mass. For a moment he thought to turn back, but then he pushed on, holding his hand out for protection, weeds picking at his sleeves, branches scratching his legs. A dog howled from somewhere in the mist, and then something moved in the trees. Demons live in trees...rather unlikely, but all the same it'll—finally, the end of the path.

Chapter XXIX

The house of Eberhard rose forebodingly out of the darkness, palisaded by a thicket of prickly underbrush, divulging no sign of life, and yet compelling the visitor to its entrance. By the looks of the door (made from a dark red wood with a heavy wolf's head knocker) it was a habitation of great antiquity. Above the knocker was a peephole, and next to that, just as the old man had described, was a bronze plate with his name on it: Bardo Thödol III. "The third?" Robert thought, rubbing dust off the plate and pondering the likelihood of such a title. And here was this name again: "Thödol." It looked German, but it didn't really sound German. And why did the old man give this name to Jürgen, but not Robert? Come to think of it, he never spoke his own name. But odder were the two sculptures in front of the door: Sphinxes; one with eyes open, and the other half closed, also looking dated. In fact, the entire house was in a state of disrepair and bore the marks of prolonged negligence.

Robert clenched his hand and to the best of his abilities announced himself in the particular way he had been instructed; but to his astonishment the door opened to his knock, unlatching and opening with a creek. The thought crossed his mind whether this was not the time to abandon this so-called meeting; if he didn't leave now he would be stuck for the duration of the old man's hospitality, and heaven knew how long that could be. For the moment he was still free. He could turn around and walk away exactly the way he came. As long as he was alone, he could simply leave with the excuse that no one had greeted him. But if he were to enter and discover Herr Eberhard hiding behind the door or innocently walking by, he would not only be bound to remain by politeness, he would be committed to an explanation of his inappropriate entry. There are moments when the body is drawn into situations where the mind is helpless, left to observe like a spectator, frightened and yet eager to see what will happen next. This was one of those moments.

As Robert's eyes began to adjust to the dark orange glow, he noticed he was in an interesting room. The entryway was in the shape of a polygon; a well-groomed, septilateral, handsomely decorated, Victorian polygon—and, as strange as this may sound, with a door on each wall. Yes, seven doors, all identical. As soon as you entered, you forgot which one you arrived through.

Dominating the room was a crystal chandelier. It was shimmering as if it had been cleaned that day, glowing in an orange haze. The walls were decorated with tasteful wallpaper and stately wood detailing. It was a dizzying example of architectural symmetry, the linear decoration seeming to bend with the rotation of the head. And the place was a striking example of domestic cleanliness. In contrast to its decayed exterior, the interior of Herr Eberhard's house was pristine.

"Choose." There came a voice, just behind Robert's ear, giving him a start, though it was whispered with quiet menace; and before he could respond, Herr Eberhard was there, motioning to the doors. "The seven metals, the seven fates, the seven heavens; the timeless moment has come."

Contrary to his usual demeanor, the old man was distant and gazing at the doors with a bizarre grimace. It looked like Herr Eberhard and yet his glassy-eyed stare was that of someone else, not unlike witnessing a friend under the influence of drugs or a loved one suffering from amnesia. Robert was becoming nervous. "But, Herr Eberhard," he said, "where did you come from?"

"The entrance to the cave; don't make him wait."

Robert paused, examining the doors, and then randomly chose one. All at once Herr Eberhard burst into his old self: "I knew it!" he cried, "You chose life! The golden Tree of Life! Partake of its fruit! For my world is now yours and my secrets will be held by your lips!"

The ecstatic outburst was just as disturbing as the calm: both suggested a volatile character. The old man swung open the door and bade Robert a hearty welcome, bowing as he did it, making a twirling gesture with his hand that ended with his arm gracefully extended in the direction of the interior. Before Robert was a long hallway lined with paintings. Upon closing the door, Robert was struck by a boldly scrawled symbol on its backside, oddly cryptic, resembling a runic symbol: winding like snakes in the form of a figure eight, open on top with a cross attached to its bottom.

"The sign of the adept," Herr Eberhard said, twisting his goatee into a spike. "Behold the spirit Mercurius, whom others call Mercury: our guide and our tempter, our good luck and our ruin, whose dual nature enables him to be not only the seventh but also the eighth, the eighth on Olympus whom nobody thought of. And the symbol you see—majestic in shape, ancient in form—is his. It's the symbol of life. And without it we cannot live."

As Herr Eberhard presented his oratory, they were walking down the corridor, which was, in fact, a portrait gallery with bronze nameplates labeling each picture: Agrippa, de Tarraga, Eleazor, Allemanno, Flamel, Trismosin, Maria Prophetissa and the Comte de Saint-Germain. One had a white rose in his hand; another was shown with a burning triangle and cross, yet another had a moon in the background. One of the portraits was of a man, sitting with his hands folded in his lap and holding a compass. The sight of this painting aroused in its beholder a most disquieting sensation of fear. In certain parts, the brush strokes were heavy and rushed as if the images were arising from a mad hellfire within the painter. In other parts, for example the eyes, the subtle shades and tones of color had been executed with such painstaking precision that the viewer was equally drawn to the conclusion that the painter had suffered in its undertaking. Around the head of the subject an almost imperceptible reddish shadow had been added, appearing as a dark halo or eminence. In striking contrast, the face was conceived with a bold, radiating brightness that brought the figure storming into the foreground. The composite effect no longer suggested a person of nobility, or even goodness, but looked exactly like a devil lunging out at his victim.

The painting absorbed Robert against his will, which in turn made it all the more repugnant, and when Herr Eberhard tapped him on the shoulder telling him to move on; he was ashamed that he had stayed so long in front of it. There were no doors along the hallway, not until the end.

Chapter XXX

"Open it and behold!" Herr Eberhard said, bowing, smiling and gesticulating in all directions. "This is the stronghold of my secrets."

The library of Herr Eberhard was square in shape with beveled corners and surrounded in the crown molding by a cryptic message. When asked what these symbols meant, Herr Eberhard turned to his pupil, and, with utmost conviction and tongue-rolling dramatic flair, spoke: "From the outer darkness of ignorance through the shadows of our earth-life winds the beautiful path of initiation into the divine light of the holy altar."

Robert smiled politely. The handsome room was furnished from floor to ceiling with oak bookcases, accented with brass and fitted with rolling ladders and little lamps that hung down like wilting flowers. The ceiling must have been five meters in height and elaborately decorated with a perspective of angels amid the clouds of a gloriously blue sky. Not far from the door was a piano, and at the far end of the room was a fireplace, crackling and popping behind an oriental screen.

Robert was impressed, and it showed in his compliments. Herr Eberhard—proving, indeed, to be a man of refined demeanor—took it all in stride with the humility of a good host, as he strolled around the room pointing out this and that volume. "We like to think of it," he mused, "as a little sanctuary of

Theosophy; a common ground for the great and varied minds of literature."

The room had almost no furniture. Only a plush reading chair, a tea tray serving as a nightstand and a unique lamp adorned with a figure of Hermes, the messenger god in mythology; all of it tastefully composed before the crackling fire. Leaning against the chair, as though it had been left there moments before, was the black cane Robert had seen at Käfer's. A pipe lay on the tray. There was a distinct sense of warmth and security in this room, far from the outside world. And, oddly enough, there were no windows and only the one door from which they had entered.

"There must be ten thousand books here," Robert commented, awestruck by the fine collection.

The old man was motionless, standing in the center of the room absorbed in thought. But starting again he vehemently exclaimed that Robert was looking at no less than twenty-three thousand six hundred seventy-two books: "A veritable cornucopia of knowledge," he said, "spilling forth its golden fruit."

"I don't know where to begin," the young guest admitted.

"Begin at the beginning, lad—Synesius, Albertus, Paracelsus and that most sacred of works and fountainhead of secrets, *The Key of Solomon.*"

"This one's over two hundred years old."

"Look here," Herr Eberhard said, drawing a dusty old tome

from the shelf. "This rare edition of *Memorabilia Urbis Wisbadenae* published in 1732 is, in my opinion, worthy of the shelves of the Pergamon. And if you look behind your shoulder you'll find an autographed first edition of poetry from the British author John Drinkwater."

Apart from the books, a peculiar aspect of the room was its paintings: imposing, finely crafted canvases, mounted in the bookcases and above the fireplace, one on each of the walls. The one above the fire was, aptly enough, a rendition of a burning bush. Upon closer inspection, a strange monster could be seen lightly painted into the flames and branches. It had the body of a dragon, a hideous snout like a wolf; and it was eating its own tail. On the other wall, above the entrance, was a dramatic depiction of a tempestuous sky with birds: a landscape without land, so to speak. In its corner, placed like a family seal, was a peacock inside of what looked like a glass gourd.

On the left wall was a scene of nymphs bathing in a pond; swimming along side them were all sorts of unusual creatures and fantastic oddities. The last and strangest of the paintings was of a towering mound of earth: terraced into levels, seven to be precise, reminiscent of an ancient ziggurat. Encompassing the mound like a rainbow were the signs of the zodiac. Inside of it was a bird spreading its wings, and in the foreground was a blindfolded man, garbed in medieval style and holding out his hand as if to catch something. When asked about the bird, Herr Eberhard mumbled something, and then promptly changed the subject.

Robert wasn't sure how to react. "This is truly the collection of a lifetime," he said, pacing from one section to another, appreciating the effort and patience required to build such a collection.

"Look," the old man whispered, moved by his pupil's enthusiasm, "these are the masters of the invisible art; that which sings without ever producing a sound, echoing in the mind as a memory of an unrealized action. This is knowledge you see. It's not easy to meet interesting people in this world. They're all too often hidden behind closed doors or confined to private communities. When we're young it seems everyone we meet is interesting; as we age, however, this number diminishes, and there's a moment when we realize it's only through their words that we make their acquaintance. These are my friends. They have shared their innermost contemplation with me, revealed their darkest secrets; and all they ask in return is time. These are individuals I could never meet in person. You will not bump into them at the park, and if you did, I fancy they wouldn't have time to spare you."

"It's true," Robert admitted, "I think I only travel so I can meet new people."

"And their words speak to us long after their bodies have gone. I find that...marvelous." Herr Eberhard allowed a pause to ensue, but it was clear this was for dramatic effect. At the moment of uttering the word "marvelous," he had brought his index finger and thumb together as if to sprinkle spice on the thought. In any case, his pupil was captivated, which signaled the command that followed: "Now Robert, go to the bookcase. Seek out the book entitled '*Zum Exedra*.' It's a thick one. You can't miss it. Find it and free it from its resting place."

Robert surveyed the room and found the book at the far end near the fireplace. Herr Eberhard, observing his apprentice's every move, spoke with utmost seriousness: "What you're about to witness, lad—the events about to unfold—you will reveal them to no one. Do you understand? Now pull the book out from the shelf. Take it—splendid! And reach into the space that remains. Reach behind the other books and feel for a lever."

"A what?" Robert entreated, reaching for anything he could get his hand on, until: "Ah yes, here it is!"—Something released from behind the bookcase and the heavy oak began to move. A track and roller system had been constructed beneath and behind it. Robert followed the instructions and found himself before a passageway. Inside was a stone staircase, leading into blackness. And there was a particular odor: a musty, dirty air, like that of a cellar, at once warm and fresh—a pungent odor, and yet Robert wasn't repelled by it. It was an odor one remembers.

"Go forth!" commanded the old man. "Go forth and cross the Rubicon!"

Chapter XXXI

The staircase was actually quite long, or so it seemed in the dark, and moved spiral-wise ever deeper, monotonously winding, as if around an unknown center, gradually getting closer to God only knew what. Herr Eberhard was mumbling to himself, something about entering the cave, going to meet "him," whatever that was supposed to mean. Robert let his hand slide against the wall as he made his descent, feeling it change from brick to stone. The air was damp, and the winding steps were slick with mildew, making it difficult to move without slipping. Moreover, it troubled Robert that he always had to walk one or two paces ahead of his host. It wasn't polite, and in a place like this it was nothing short of dangerous. Accordingly, he paused several times to let Herr Eberhard catch up, but as soon as he did the old man dropped behind again. Robert, teetering between frustration and fear, had no idea where he was being taken, or *if* he was being taken for that matter (only now did Robert realize that this meeting could have been a trap and that an ambush lay ahead). At any rate, after an indeterminate length of time, he got there.

Before them was a massive door—not rectangular in shape, but round resembling the entrance to an oriental temple. The wood had been painted dark red, and all around the edge was a black metal border in the shape of flames, in its center a large ring-shaped handle. But who in the world would invest such time and effort into such a thing? Next to the door was a torch, which Herr Eberhard lit setting everything aglow. Far off, echoing deep within the darkness, was the sound of dripping water, and a hollow moan of machinery could be heard reverberating in distant passages, hinting at the size of this labyrinth. How far underground had they gone? And who had scratched those designs into the rock? One appeared to be a devil, dancing in the flickering light of the torch.

The master ordered his apprentice to open the weighty door (not for a moment considering his pupil could be frightened by what lay behind it). It opened with a creak and a burst of white light from the room within. It was a striking room: semicircular in shape with a domed ceiling, three rows of seats, all in marble, and a wooden podium at the front. There was a mural of seven figures standing around a fountain in discussion, all of them draped in white togas except one wearing red and holding a cup with three snakes.

Just then, Herr Eberhard placed a white cloth in Robert's hand, asking him to put it on. If Robert had been paying attention to all the peculiar biddings of this visit, he wouldn't have cared about this one. Be that as it may, his first reaction was to refuse, adding that playing Caesar was going a bit far. The old man just about came apart at the seams.

"Look me in the eye," he roared, "look at me and say the noble raiment of Plato is silly! It's blasphemous what you suppose! Shamelessly unorthodox! Heresy in the highest measure!"

Robert tried to put on the toga, which was actually a complicated process. While the right hand held one end of the cloth, the left knee had to be lifted to get the other end under the groin and around the waist properly. Meanwhile, the left hand was kept busy trying to drape the cloth over the right shoulder. Once he got it on, however, with his master's help, it was comfortable.

"Good," the old man said, tucking in a piece of cloth, "now take a seat...take a seat, boy. We haven't got all night."

"What are you talking about, Herr Eberhard?"

"The lecture, by Jove! You don't think I've invited you here for tea, do you? The moment of enlightenment is upon us. The Master of Secrets has promised to speak. He will be here within moments. Sit! There! Sit, sit!"

Robert took a seat and waited. Herr Eberhard sat down next to him and stared into space, perfectly silent, leaving Robert no choice, but to follow his lead. He tried to imagine what he looked like dressed in a toga, seated in this room, waiting for a lecture, sometime after midnight on Friday while the rest of the world was leading a normal life. The rest of the world...it felt distant. His attention fell upon a door near the podium, and, after a time, the expected occurred; it began to open.

Robert's first reaction was to jump when he saw what entered the room. The door opened and an impressive, great body made its entrance—at least two meters in height, of tremendous stature, having to bend down as it passed through the doorway. Herr Eberhard appeared mesmerized by the ominous form, murmuring repeatedly: "The mystagogue."

He—or better still, "it"—was dressed completely in black, in a hooded robe that fell to the floor, secured around his waist with a piece of rope lending him the comportment of a giant monk. He was holding a long black cane fitted with an ivory effigy of a frog, similar in style to that of Herr Eberhard's with the sarcophagus. On his right hand was a thick gold ring. Even more conspicuous was the scraggly gray beard jutting out from his prognathous face—a genuine bush, reminding Robert of— but of course! The Russian chapel!

Without speaking, the formidable figure nodded in the direction of Herr Eberhard. He then turned to Robert, held out his fist, extending his arm until it was completely erect pointing at Robert, and opened his hand wide, holding this position for some twenty seconds of ringing silence. Spellbound, Robert looked into the weathered palm, ploughed with cracks and crevices, and at length the daunting figure retracted, bringing its fingers together in the shape of a triangle, and nodded to Robert.

"A magical event," Herr Eberhard whispered excitedly, nudging his apprentice with enthusiasm. "He's recognized you! And he's promised us to discuss the water."

"Us?"

The mysterious figure approached the podium, held both

hands in the air, and, with an intensity to part a sea, spoke: "...*és amint Isten keze megérintette a Földet, hatalmas víztömeg tört elő a Föld mélyéből. A víz, amit iszunk, egy nap minket fog elnyelni. De ha megtaláljuk a forrást, eljön az örök fiatalság...*"

Robert sat through the entire lecture, and inasmuch as he couldn't understand a word from the mysterious tongue—indeed, it was like watching a foreign film without subtitles—he focused on its rhythm and intonation. The words flowed from the mouth with an oriental pitch, at once deeply guttural and sharply nasal, although, despite their unintelligible origins, the individual syllables rang clear. The voice was rough and grave, projecting the sounds with weight, and yet there was a singing quality to it, curiously pleasing to the ear and oddly melodic. Robert looked over to Herr Eberhard sitting next to him and watched his face as it reacted to the sounds in the air. Sometimes he smiled in total agreement, and then a moment later he appeared to be in the depths of concentration. At a certain level, it was an enjoyable experience. For there is an instinctive sense in all of us that can feel the meanings of unintelligible tongues.

"Incontestably true!" Herr Eberhard exclaimed, rising out of his seat and throwing his hands in the air. "Bravo! A paragon of theory that strives for empyrean! I excuse myself, if I shed a tear of gratitude for the knowledge I've received. By Jove, the Elixir of Life...genius! Come, let us meet him."

They approached the imposing figure at the podium at which point Herr Eberhard presented Robert with all the pomp and circumstance of a young prince. "It is with the humblest intentions," he said, bowing practically to the floor, "that I present to you the one who has caught the attention of so many in our community here in Wiesbaden...Herr Holsen."

Robert hesitated as he tried to recall when he told Herr Eberhard his family name, but it was already too late. The large, dark man, towering head and shoulders above the others, approached as if to shake hands, but instead grabbed Robert, giving him a hug: "You shall complete the *ternarius,*" he declared in his uniquely exotic tone and accent so thick the words were scarcely comprehensible. Up close, the subhuman, octave-low voice was even more impressive, sending a chill down Robert's spine: "I am Király," (pronounced 'Kee-rye') "son of Mithras, brother of Sirona, resident of the ancient city of Aquincum located in the outskirts of Obuda." The overwhelming presence of this man would have sent most people running, but Robert admirably kept his composure.

With hands held out in the air, the mystagogue closed his eyes and continued in his eerie Nosferatu voice: "And a river went out of Eden to water the garden; and from thence it was parted, and became into four heads. The name of the first is *Pi'-son*: that is it which compasseth the whole land of *Hav'-i-lah,* where there is gold."

"I'm sorry," Robert apologized, clearing his throat, "I don't really understand what—"

"You... are... he," the shadowy mass proclaimed.

"Dear boy," interrupted Herr Eberhard going to open the second door and bidding his companions to enter, "we must push on before starting such pertinent discussions."

Robert, in confusion, turned to Herr Eberhard, and then back to the frightening man.

"YOU... ARE... HE."

Chapter XXXII

The heavy door closed with an echoing slam, and all was dark again in the tunnels of this vertiginous domain. Space was tight in the musty shaft, and Robert could sense that he was descending: "Herr Eberhard," he said, nervously grasping into the air, for the old man was propelling him from behind, "you really should be leading. I have no idea where we're supposed to be going."

"Yes yes, a labyrinth of doubt," the old man laughed fiendishly, pushing his guest into the darkness, "a curious excursion into the ageless soul; and once you've made the difficult and complicated journey, what is at the center? You are!"

Now the surroundings were more like a mineshaft than like a tunnel: the walls were hewn of stone, the ground was flat and grainy. After some twenty meters, lighted by a flickering lamp, there was a junction. Pointing left was an arrow labeled *Kurhaus*; pointing right: *Aquis Laboratorium*. Herr Eberhard, putting his hand on Robert's shoulder and squeezing, proclaimed that this was one of his greatest secrets.

Robert pulled back. "That's not what I think it is, is it?"

"Yes," he said, "direct access to the Kurhaus."

"I meant the other sign."

"With it, I never have to enter Käfer's from the front door."

Herr Király had a disapproving look on his face, and pointed to the other arrow. Herr Eberhard ignored his colleague, intoxicated with the thrill of bringing a newcomer into this tortuous network of tunnels and rooms: "The wars," he said, pointing into the darkness, "fear built this. It's defensive in nature, cowardice in the face of defeat, a retreat to the earth from which we came."

"Do you mean this is all some kind of bomb shelter?"

The old man was pleased. "When I arrived in 1952, the landlord told me it was the cellar. Imagine that! Much work was invested in returning it to its functional state. Luckily, I was still young."

"And this actually leads all the way to the Kurhaus?"

"The tunnel system," Herr Eberhard went on, "is considerably larger than it appears. The earliest passageways, such as the one that led us down to the exedra, date back to the time of the Kurdirektor Heyl."

"The guy on the statue in the Kurpark?"

"Yes, an interesting man. He believed he would live longer

by avoiding pollen in spring. By his final days, the poor fellow was avoiding people as well."

"And he lived in this house?"

Herr Eberhard nodded affirmatively, explaining that at the time of his terrestrial departure, Heyl owned the entire residence, gardens, servant's quarters, guest bungalow and a laboratory devoted to the study of rheumatoid arthritis: "The laboratory is no longer standing, and the house has been subsequently divided over the years. Only the lower levels are in my possession today."

"But that can't be the end," commented Robert, inspecting some shiny flecks in the wall.

"You're right, it is not." And then the old man told a story. "Upon the death of Herr Kurdirektor Heyl, the great Herr Professor Fresenius leapt upon the chance to acquire the residence. Fresenius was a renowned advocate of the aquatic arts, and followed the labor of Heyl for years before the two supposedly had a terrible falling out. Fresenius founded the Wiesbaden Institute of Chemical Research, which, incidentally, bears his name to this day and is the center of hydrological research in the region. Now, here is where the story becomes odd. No sooner had Fresenius moved in, than the reporting of paranormal phenomena began. Wiesbaden's academic community didn't know how to react. Some contended the hallucinations were due to Fresenius' age; others suspected the Heyl family was plotting against him for having taken their home; and still others said he just went nuts. Regardless of the truth, the sightings continued and inside of a year Fresenius had spilled his absinthe!" by that expression meaning that he was dead.

Herr Eberhard pulled in close and whispered: "Publicly, he was said to have passed away in his sleep. Privately, neighbors reported screams coming from the lonely house. A funeral was held and Fresenius' reputation was saved, although no one ever actually saw the body. Rumor has it that he did not die in his sleep, but somewhere here in the tunnels. It has been said that he was buried alive, attempting to find the point at which the twenty-six subterranean rivers of Wiesbaden converge. His assistant, who reputedly spoke with him days before his disappearance, swore Fresenius predicted his own death. Supposedly, he said that the waters of Wiesbaden were, and I use his exact words here, 'heated by hell itself', and that we 'must not try to seek its origins'. But, of course, we know this is only hearsay. Regardless of the fate of our dear Fresenius, he did manage during his short residence here at Parkstrasse 3 to extend the tunnels began by Heyl. Today this arm of the system bears his name: *Die Fresenius Passage.*"

"And did he ever find the meeting point?"

"Of the rivers?" our host challenged, "Of course not! A great construction may be functional, but a beautiful one is invariably useless. Nothing destroys beauty like function."

For a long time already Robert had been hearing a noise coming from the tunnel, a droning chug not unlike a tired old steam engine, but he didn't feel right to ask. Herr Király pointed to the arrow a second time and Herr Eberhard, nodding to his silent colleague, called for the tour to continue. The three started again down the passage in the opposite direction of the Kurhaus, and for the first time Herr Király let a smile cross his face.

Everything was dark except the lamps passing overhead. The air dampened, the temperature cooled, and the peculiar odor of earlier had returned, becoming stronger as they continued. Herr Eberhard was humming to himself; a tune Robert couldn't recognize. Somehow the presence of Herr Király provided a feeling of security; and contrary to Robert's first impression of the man, there was something gentle about him.

The ominous figure motioned for the other two to pause for a moment in front of the large steel portal that was now before them. It was a door right out of a Jules Verne novel. Around its edges were thick rivets, and its hinges must have been as big as footballs. In its center was a wheel like one would imagine from a submarine. Herr Király grabbed it with both hands, and gave it an arduous jerk. Nothing happened. He had to attempt this three times before successfully freeing the rusty mechanism with a loud, shrill squeak that blared deep into the tunnels, losing itself in distant shafts and hollows. One would have thought the thing was rarely opened, but the two hosts seemed familiar with the operation. Once it had been cracked, Herr Király let out a wild laugh of accomplishment. Herr Eberhard was gleaming with delight.

Chapter XXXIII

The room Robert entered was unlike anything he had ever seen. All around were large aluminum tanks, like those found in beer breweries; water was dripping everywhere. There was a jungle of pipes spreading in all directions, and puddles on the floor; but, most striking of all, was the air, thick with the sweet and pungent odor of minerals. Robert touched one of the tanks; it was cold and rusty, condensation visible on its surface; another was warm with calcium deposit around the faucets. The odor, rich in the essence of cooked egg, distinctly resembled that of the Kochbrunnen, only stronger.

"Quick, breathe deeply," commanded the old man. "Can you smell it?"

"You mean the egg?" Robert asked.

"The Spirit!"

As one walked around, the scents continually changed: sometimes earthy, other times rusty, and still others sulphurous. Along the back wall was what looked like a hearth and a large black cauldron, filled with something bubbling and popping like soup; and next to that a bellow to stoke the fire.

Herr Eberhard held out his hands. "Behold the world of Hydrology."

"Hi-what?"

"Hydrology!" cried our host, delivering his lecture not merely with hand and voice, but his entire body: "The scientific observation and documentation of all things aquatic—liquid life! The third element. The noble discipline that traces its roots to the earliest experimentation of Hippocrates 400 years before the birth of Christ. It was he who brought to the pages of Western history the observation that not all water is the same: *aluminis, bituminis, nitri, salis*. He who laid the foundations for the theories of Plinius 400 years later."

A pipe burst, spewing out steam and wildly hissing. Robert jumped. Herr Király recoiled, holding his hands in the air making the gesture of a magician casting a spell. Herr Eberhard continued speaking, unaffected: "Robert, disrobe and put on the smock to your left. You may place the toga in the cubbyhole next to the rack."

Robert noticed his name had been embroidered onto the smock. It was clear this was part of some weird plan; however the question remained, why. Robert knew he ought to retaliate, put a stop to this game once for all, but everything was happening too quickly, the speed of this fatuous trek was disorienting him, and with each new chamber reality was distanced yet again. Herr Eberhard, with the charm of a mad scientist, only made things worse, bent on adding fuel to the fire.

"Look about you," he said, approaching one of the tanks and caressing it like a thoroughbred. "Behold the tanks that contain the sacred fluid that breathes life into this land. Twenty-six in number! Brilliant nephritic vesicles of metal: isolating, cleansing and purifying the waters of this blessed region. Each tank represents one of the original springs; flowing before Goth and Frank ever locked horns in combat, Celt and Roman shook hands in agreement. It's time itself, contained in liquid form!"

"Does anyone know of this?"

"Go to that tank there on your left and read its nameplate."

Robert approached the tank, examined it and called out "Adlerquelle." Herr Eberhard congratulated the response, though our exhausted hero had no recollection of ever seeing a source with this name. And yet it was revealed that Robert did know of this water; as a matter of fact, he knew of it intimately. It was no less than one of the "Principle Three," whatever that was supposed to mean. By the way Herr Eberhard spoke these words, one could sense the importance they held for him. And no sooner had these words entered Robert's vocabulary came two more of even greater importance: "*Aquae Mattiacorum.*" Robert could please his mentor only as far as divining that these terms had something to do with the ancient Romans who had once occupied Wiesbaden.

"A promethean deduction!" exclaimed Herr Eberhard, looking over to his colleague and winking. "Naturally, our blackhaired bearers of civilization." He made his way through the wet room until he was standing directly before one of the metallic tanks. A glass of water had made its way to his hand, and after drinking it down in a single gulp, the pedagogue spoke: "The moment of truth has come. Wiesbaden, known as *Aquae*

Mattiacorum to those in the community, developed around three principle calorific springs. The first of the three, you discovered early on in your adventures here: it is, of course, the Kochbrunnen. What you may not have known is that you've been under the scrutiny of our select network ever since you took the first sip! What may also be new to your ears is that no more than a meter beneath the boiling fountain are the foundations of a Roman bathing complex. Archaeological excavations undertaken in the first years of the last century brought to light no less than six baths with heated floors and changing rooms. Later, through privately funded research, evidence of human remains was identified in the surrounding stratigraphic layers, and recently in the water itself. For want of a better term to describe this numinous union with the dead, you've been drinking Romans!"

"I think I feel sick," moaned Robert.

"We're convinced the spirits are surfacing at this point," the old man continued with flawless objectivity, "We've collected many accounts of sightings around the Kochbrunnen, and all who visit it swear to have felt an indescribable presence."

"And now ghosts?"

"In particular, the Roman goddess of healing *Hygieia*, Wife of the Steam. Rumor has it the Kochbrunnen is her favorite of Aquae Mattiacorum's sources; and—I just mention this in passing—it's said she has an affinity to the sick at heart. We've heard folkloric tales of her materializing amidst the vapors and guiding the passionate—sometimes to happiness, sometimes to sorrow. Like many goddesses, she is capricious and whimsical."

"It just doesn't sound true."

"But lad, just as good fiction never sounds false, good reality never sounds true." Yes, the old man was on a roll, and it was apparent his pupil was beginning to see the light. Robert couldn't help himself from wanting to know more, asking questions about this place and that, demanding details and begging clarification, eagerly absorbing every thought like a sponge. All the while, Herr Eberhard was pacing up and down the lab, noting facts, pointing out figures and elucidating his subject in a clear and plastic prose: "The second principle source," he continued, designating one of the tanks, "you've also discovered. It's called the *Schützenhofquelle*. Of the three, we believe it to possess the strongest aura, and to this day it's protected by *Sirona*: the goddess of healing. Test excavations suggest it's the oldest of the three, and it was here that in 1783 our forefathers discovered the dedication stone to the God of healing *Apollo Toutiorix*. The primordial energy around this source is tremendous. A veritable convergence point! You discovered it late in your adventures here and didn't realize the amplifying affect it had on your experience. It was the last of the three you discovered. And it wasn't until this moment that you succumbed to the mysterious powers that have kept us all here."

"Now wait a minute, you said it was the last of the three I discovered? So, the second must be...the *Bäckerbrunnen?*" The old man shook his head negatively. "*The Faulbrunnen?*"

"No, boy. You bathed in it."

"I bathed in it?"

Herr Eberhard nodded. "The third principle source bears the name you've just spoken: *Adlerquelle.* Of the three Roman bath complexes it's the central, and we believe the purest, leading those in our community to place particular value on its curative affects. The name, which obviously is not Latin, rises out of the Dark Ages at which time one of the earliest bathhouses of the post-Roman era was constructed around it: the hotel '*Adler,*' or 'Eagle' in your language. This establishment continued to heal the weak into the renaissance and from thereon down through the early modern era; as far as the turn of the century, 1899 to be precise, when it was decided to reconstruct the complex as the 'Central Cure Building,' which eventually took the name by which we recognize it today: *Kaiser Friedrich Bad.*"

"You mean where Jürgen took me?"

"Yes, it was at this second phase in your adventures here that, without your knowledge of the act, you severed the ties to your home, your friends and the life that couldn't bring you fulfillment. By letting go and taking the plunge, by having dipped in the Bain-marie, your spirit was lifted and the forty-nine day cycle was begun. This was your rebirth! Your baptism into balneological enlightenment! For every time one swims, one experiences the womb; we are made of water and to return to it is to return to ourselves. This is the reason we feel younger as the result. You needed the guidance of our friend, Jürgen, a young apprentice in our ranks who has not progressed at the rate with which you have impressed so many here. Yes, boy, we asked him to take you."

Robert stared at the old man. Was he to believe that Jürgen was part of some plot against him? That everything that had thus far happened was not of his own free will? And about the true nature of this plan and about its instigator was he to learn nothing?

Herr Eberhard was clearly deriving a perverse joy from Robert's discoveries. His voice was trembling with ecstasy, on the verge of a wild laugh. "But you must realize your progress has been extraordinary! Perfect enlightenment is at your heels! You're becoming who you are!"

"My progress?" Robert pleaded, pressing his temples with both hands. "Becoming who I am?"

"Of course," the master said outright. "And this is no easy task. For once we have chosen ourselves, all other possibilities are ruled out. So many rely on choice—they flee into dreams of options and chance—so few deny it and rely on themselves. We've all got accustomed to making do with other people's intelligence; but it's better to be your own fool than someone else's parrot! Look to the world and find the world; look to yourself and find genius! And the only way to do this is by casting choice away! Now go to the tank there on your right... yes, that one, good. Look at the nameplate. Read it to us—yes, that one, the one on top. Tell us what it says."

"It says *Faulbrunnen.*"

The old man never looked happier. "Precisely!" he cheered. "Now go to the sink over there. Look inside. Yes. There's a container filled with water. No, not the alembic, and certainly not the cucurbit—yes, that's it! Pick it up. Good. Now hold it up to the light and tell us what you see."

"Well," he said, "It's the color green."

"Bravo!" cried the host, slapping his knee. "Luster of the Green Lion! You've got it!"

"At the risk of being rude, Herr Eberhard; so what?"

"Do you think every town in Europe has green water?"

"I heard London does," Robert mused, but the more he resolved not to show fear, the more plainly one could see it in his voice and manner.

The old man pursed his lips and thought for a moment, watching Robert like a hawk. Then he grinned: "A clever display of witticism, young thespian, heartily I laugh with you—indeed, I am grateful for your humor—however the answer is no. What you witness is an occurrence unique to Wiesbaden. A mineral composition found nowhere else on the planet. Remarkable enough, my dear fellow, to have brought me here from a place of safety in the south of Moravia, and the good Herr Király all the way from the Carpathian Basin; a land endowed with a plethora of aquatic sources."

Herr Király gave a confirmatory nod.

"And if I can ask," Robert continued, nearing the end of his rope, "what is so special about the water here?"

Herr Eberhard approached him, looked around as if someone were listening in, and, in a grave and dour tone, revealed what he thought to be one of his greatest secrets: "Hydrological analyses suggest it's curative."

"You mean it's healthy," Robert said.

"No lad, we mean it's curative."

"But this can't possibly be unique to Wiesbaden's water."

To this the old man practically exploded, letting off a cannonade of references to every medicinal fountain west of the Volga, uncontrollably speechifying and passionately bellowing, as if Robert had thrown his life's reputation into question: "Boy, do you think your present company are amateur drinkers? Do you think we do this for fun? We've strolled the colonnades of Karlovy Vary, floated in the calorific pools of Heviz, drank from the Pump Room of Bath, aye, tested the springs of Spa itself. But Wiesbaden—it is unique! This fluid is singular! It's unique in its relationship to the organism. We believe it to be psychosomatic in nature."

"A placebo?"

"No, on the contrary: an elixir. Do you realize we may have stumbled upon *the* Arcanum here: Mercury's fountain, the Water of Life, a panacea of the purest extraction. In short, the most beautiful, potent, unsullied *medicine* we've ever seen. What I wish to say is it appears to show evidence of rejuvenation."

"You mean it's healthy," Robert said once again.

"No, no," moaned the old man. Robert had reiterated his question out of an honest attempt at following his host's idea; all the same it could have been construed as ironical, and Herr Eberhard flared up as if he had been slapped. "It's not as simple as that," he said curtly. "The lithium concentration alone can kill if ingested in excess."

"It's poisonous?"

"Yes," replied the old man, with a slight change in voice, "like a vaccine. But don't let this frighten you. For it's surely a miracle that in a venomous dragon there should be the great Medicine: the *Uroboros*, Robert—the lizard that devours its noxious tail. And if I have called this toxic draft a cure, I did so only after mature consideration and a careful appraisal of the empirical and historical data. But I don't wish to labor this argument longer, for such an interpretation lies beyond my powers of proof."

"You're not sure it's good for us?"

"We believe it to be."

"Is faith enough?"

The old man, who was now bending over the sink washing out a vial, merely turned his head and said calmly, in striking contrast to the confused stuttering and jabbering of Robert: "We must keep drinking."

Robert was not in the least satisfied with this answer. Everything he was learning was deeply inspirational and yet poison to his own good judgment. Accordingly, his logical faculties were in an uproar. "But what if it hurts you?" he pleaded.

"That's a part of it, my boy."

"I just don't get it."

"I know. You find my ideas obscure. Alas, you're not alone. However, I am prepared to explain them to you—yes, you have earned this privilege—and to the best of my ability. I may not be mistaken in supposing that this is what you came for. Well, by all means!"

Chapter XXXIV

The old man turned off the faucet, wiped his hands and walked right up to Robert's face. "Boy," he said, in total earnestness, "the sages will tell you that two fishes swim in our sea, without any flesh or bones. *This* is what we're after. Let them be cooked in their own water; for then and only then will they become a vast sea, the vastness of which no man can describe. The secret appears to lie in the relationship of these two fishes, spirit and soul; and it is possible that the sulphurous liquid flowing from the Kochbrunnen, this magnificent transforming draft, is the missing link. Do you realize there are mountainous lands where the inhabitants live forever? We believe this is happening here as well. Verily, if we told you our age, you wouldn't believe us." The old man, keenly observing his pupil, cleared his throat. "There is an ancient Tibetan book which describes a period of wandering that all men must one day face. It is a journey like no other, and it lasts forty-nine days. We believe you are on this path, the path of the adept, unaware and yet fixed on your target. It is a voyage into perfect enlightenment. And we would like to help you reach it. Now, it's an established fact that bonds exist between the organic brain and the incorporeal thoughts it creates; that one influences the other and vice versa, as it were. Much exploration has been made into influencing the body by way of the mind: healing through meditation, suppression of chronic disease, hypnosis and the like. What has yet to be considered, though, is the potential of their conjunction. Yes, we mean to say the union of tissue and thought, the marriage of body to spirit and soul, a wedding of the trinity that defines us. The core of the matter is thus: the water in this laboratory appears to exert a quantifiable influence on the gray matter itself; and if this is the case, then it's possible that the thoughts are equally being impacted. The fishes are being cooked! By heating up the sea the three become the one!"

"You wish to control the relationship between body and soul?" asked Robert, sincerely trying to follow this outlandish train of thought: "But, why?"

"To end them," said the old man without batting an eyelid.

"Don't you see? It's youth we're after! And the Kochbrunnen could be its fountain; Wiesbaden, Shangri-La."

"The fountain of youth? Here? Now you've gone too far!"

"Hold your horses, and look before you choose not to leap. No daring speculation or extravagant fancy is needed to see the affect this water has on the body. To the best of my experience we are dealing here with a uniquely curative compound. And, on my honor, I assure you that the research carried out in this household is of the utmost scientific standards. Do you think the bounty of the adept comes without the disbelief of the layman? It has always been this way."

"But how, then?"

"Robert, life, as you and I know it, is the act of our bodies' cells replenishing themselves. Please be so good as to approach the table there on your left, look into the microscope—yes, peer into the Eye of Allah—and behold reality. We live as long as we produce cells, and when this process ceases to continue, we cease to exist. Now, as we get older, the rate of cell replenishment in our bodies slows down. This is aging. Are you following me thus far? Very well, then, here we go: specific areas of the human chromosome are implicated in the aging process. We call the genes from this area 'transposons'. And, by Jove, they're responsible for regulating the rate of replenishment. In essence, they're the genes that code for the regulation of the process of cellular replenishment."

"I think I just lost you," pleaded Robert, gasping for

intellectual air. Once having tapped into his beloved subject, however, the old man couldn't be stopped.

"Let us return to our sacred Kochbrunnen," he said. "I suppose you've examined the Chemical Analysis posted next to the source itself."

"Yes, I even wrote it down in my notes."

"Good. And did you notice the presence of arsenic in your nectar?"

"Actually, I did, but isn't that a poison?"

"Yes, if ingested in excess. If taken in regulated doses, however, the body can adopt it. It's well known in history that kings and kaisers have become immune to it."

"And what does arsenic have to do with living longer?"

"A piercing question, my pupil. You see it's the only substance that contains the element responsible for interruption of the electron transport chain in human oxidative phosphorylation. That's the poison's secret! All that's left is to distil it, and we have the *prima materia*: the arcane substance, which is the elixir!"—The old man was crazed with certitude, clenching his fists and sweating profusely, storming across the room throwing switches and madly turning dials—"So as not to burden this exposition unduly, I exercise the greatest reserve in summarizing our unorthodox discoveries. In short, research carried out in this laboratory suggests that if the body successfully reacts with the Kochbrunnen-Arsenic, it can potentially inhibit the mechanism responsible for production of the chemical that slows down the rate of replenishment in our golden years through what we call 'feedback inhibition'. Now it is, as I can hardly refrain from remarking, a curious sport of nature that the water, which is toxic, is affecting the transposons and causing the body to build an immunity to aging!"

"I don't know. It just doesn't seem likely."

"But look at the era we're in! Our societies are progressing at a rate that time itself is becoming redundant. We're accelerating! And it's here in this household where we take an active interest in the adaptation of our organisms to this change in temporality. This is the time we're in! Can you understand that?"

"It has become clear, Herr Eberhard," Robert explained in that strangely calm voice that precedes a nervous breakdown, "indeed, very clear, that I no longer know exactly what time I'm in. I mean, of course, I know what the calendar year is; but it has been increasingly difficult to discern the era."

"Hmm, indeed," remarked the old man, squeezing his brow and biting his tongue in thought.

"For instance," Robert continued, "does architecture not play a greater role in our environment than time? Is Frankfurt not further into the future than Wiesbaden?"

The old man sighed deeply: "A textbook example, yes," and motioned for his colleague to fetch a notebook. "Do you ever find yourself overcome with tiredness, lad?"

"Why yes, there are days when all I can do is sleep."

Herr Eberhard turned to Herr Király, handed him a pen and

whispered in his ear: "Clearly showing signs of it, yes."

"Signs of what?" snapped Robert.

"Please," said the old man, who as soon as Robert raised his voice grew calm, indeed almost rueful, and thus contrived either to confuse his guest or to some extent bring him to his senses. By the pained manner in which he cleared his throat and pathetically smiled, it was apparent the tidings weren't good: "Are you familiar, boy, with the condition known as 'Temporal Disconnection'?"

"Temporal what?"

"Quite common," he explained, signaling for his colleague to begin recording. "Many of us suffer from it."

"I studied archaeology for seven years and never heard of such malarkey!" protested Robert in a voice that testified to his jangled nerves. All the while, the oversized monk was busily scribbling down every word.

Herr Eberhard, retaining his cool demeanor, turned to Herr Király a second time and mumbled something: "Yes yes, but no less than delta phase—Robert, quick, what time is it? How long have we been in this house?"

"It's—I, I don't know."

Herr Király marked something on a piece of paper as Herr Eberhard dictated in the voice of a Swiss psychotherapist. "Have you ever had the feeling you were possessed?" he asked; and when his patient replied in the negative, he posed the question further: "And that you could have lived in another era?"

"Of course," Robert affirmed, "doesn't everybody?"

"And that an earlier era rests within you?"

"Isn't that due to movies?"

Herr Eberhard held out his hand to Robert's forehead, and spoke to his colleague: "It looks like we have a case of Atavism to boot—type B, predominantly genealogical, with a rising cultural element." Again, Herr Király wrote something down in his notebook, and then Herr Doktor continued: "Yes, I knew it. The two often go hand in hand. As you may well know, it's an established fact of nature that certain traits, phenotypes if you will, appear to show the ability to lay dormant for generations at a time, and then suddenly express themselves long after the original bearer has passed on. It is these recessive, or complimentary, genes that interest us so in this household."

"And what in God's green earth does all this have to do with me?" Robert demanded, becoming frantic and not aware of his volume.

The old man, holding his diagnostic tone, made no attempt to placate him. "It's clear that you carry in yourself the spirit of a generation gone by; not your parents', possibly your grandparents', perhaps earlier. What I'm saying, my admirable apprentice, is that this nostalgia you try to suppress is part of your nature. It's a link in the chain from which you are made."

Frustration turned to anger, and Robert shouted: "I consider myself more modern than a lot of people!"

"And you are, but that has nothing to do with what we are saying."

Robert cracked. This last remark finally awakened all the outrage that had been festering within him since he first met this man: "And for God's sake," he screamed, "what are you saying? Will someone tell me? You've walked me through your house like some kind of mentally retarded child! Dressed me up in a toga! And now in this stupid lab jacket! You speak in languages I can't understand! Diagnose me with diseases I've never heard of! You speak of Romans like they were still with us! Speak of genetics like it was psychology! History like it was philosophy! Constantly using words I can't even pronounce, let alone understand! You always answer my questions with more questions! You speak of other invisible people like we were being watched! And worst of all, unbelievable as this all sounds, you do it with smiles on your faces! You keep guiding me along like I'm enjoying all this! You hold some sort of carrot before me that I'm unable to avoid following! You're playing with me, I tell you! Playing with me like a puppet! And all I ask of you, over and over, is that you explain what you want so desperately for me to learn! What are you saying? What in the name of God are you saying?"

Herr Király approached Robert and handed him a glass: one filled with an unusual liquid; swirls of pearly green sediment in a rich, argentiferous syrup, bubbling and steaming like lava, speckled with grain and shiny flakes. The impressive figure cast a regard of deepest gravity; and yet a strange satisfaction, almost paternal, radiated from the ancient face.

"You have not come from the solid land," he said, "but from the ceaseless void of the heavens, across the great body of water, touching down on new and fertile soil, in search of us. And yet how could you find us if you had yet to discover yourself? Your soul is a vessel, abandoned on the infinite sea of desires, amid the mirages of knowledge and the unreason of the world—a craft at the mercy of the sea's great madness, unless it throws out a solid anchor, faith, or raises its spiritual sails so that the breath of God may bring it to port. You had not yet sought yourself, and you found us. Now we bid you lose us and find yourself; and only then will we return to you."

The three became silent. And within the silence, the chaos dissipated. Herr Eberhard took Robert's hand, and for the first time looked dead serious. His eyes seemed to say that he had long foreseen this moment, and that it was no mild task to witness its realization. Herr Király stood with head tilted down. Without a word, Robert brought the glass to his lips…

…and drank.

PART FOUR

Rubedo

Chapter XXXV

The Taunusstrasse was smothered by an oppressively cold air: an air that stung the cheeks and made the nose run: an air that consumed life and stripped trees of foliage. There was no snow on the ground, no rain and no sun—only a relentless, biting cold that hung over the city like a shroud. It was a morning the working world would never know: an unearthly atmosphere created by the absence of people, a virgin landscape violated only by the one transgressing it. The only sound were his steps, echoing claps muffled by the damp air; accompanied by the beating of his heart, thumping in his chest to the point of palpitation.

The Parsival was empty. It, too, had been touched by this frosty atmosphere. And yet—he rubbed his eyes and let his face come near to the window. He pressed his temples and looked again. Seated in the corner, alone with coffee and postcard, was a man; the only one without a partner, the outsider. His body had been transported to this place, and yet his life remained in another. That is why he was writing, and why he looked away when the blonde in the awning chair attempted to catch his eye; but as he ran through that moment in his mind, he began to sense an aura of hitherto unknown awareness: she was with friends, in a familiar environment, enjoying the repose of a harmonious existence. Her body and life were one. Not until now had this metamorphosis effected its spell to the degree that this man in the café, with his myriad emotions of hope and despair, had become unknowable.

It had been some time since he had taken a solitary walk; a much needed life assessment. Some call this a reality check, others taking stock; that is, these moments when we attempt the formidable task of defining our place in the structure of life and its manifold webs that constitute our existence. We aspire to separate from ourselves, poke our heads out from the fog of uncertainty, tear away the veil of ignorance, in liberation from the individual perspective of reality, and look back in curiosity. Moments of the actualization that we are trapped in our bodies, that we will die; and as the pressure of life builds, or at least our misunderstanding of it, we periodically require these moments in which we allow the brain to reorganize the data. The task is best carried out alone, and rhythmic physical exertion aids the process: a walk—not advice, and certainly not philosophy, but a walk. He drew a deep breath, held it for a few moments and then exhaled. The sensation was pleasurable. He liked to hold his breath; these sublime instants when the metabolic rhythm is broken and all is still save the beating of the heart; like being underwater, immersed in aqueous silence, when we experience serenity that must be similar to death.

Where could this be?—this equivocal terrain that seemed to bisect the town like a prism, creating a mirror-like border between reality and dream. The sidewalk was clean, leaves were raked, windows shined and bushes were groomed, but not a soul was in sight. The entire scene emitted the beauty of a well-preserved corpse: a sparkling past that had lost its bond to the present, a proud old gadget that had outlived its usefulness without having lost its charm. Measureless energy spent on events that seemed unreal; events that showed no connection to the path life had thus far unfolded. And yet, for the first time, he experienced what he believed to be a mystical occurrence. This was not to say a bolt of lightning or crash of thunder signaling an epiphany capable of changing life in an instant. Nor was it mere superstition, which, acute by definition, is no more than an insult when pitted against the timeless unknown. And it was certainly not some corner of the parietal lobe going numb for a few instants of out-of-body elation. No, this was something brewing; something that had slipped in undetected and had slowly taken over, profound in nature and sure to have a lasting influence. It was not affecting what he saw, but his relationship to what he was seeing, teaching him to feel in ways never before tapped, believing in things he had always known to be true, and yet habitually denied.

It was just ahead, that most secret fountain of health, flowing as it had since the dawn of time, spewing forth its steaming currents that healed some and brought others to darkest perdition, calling forth its thirsty child, inviting him to partake of its iniquitous milk. He had veered off the Taunusstrasse and was heading toward the Kranzplatz where the divine liquid surfaced, along the street where the Klappe is located; the place where the other had met Petra and alluded to things better left unsaid. She would surely object to this situation. Even worse, maybe she was right; perhaps this was all nothing more than the fruits of mendacious devilry: a grand false belief or a tragic flight of fancy—a delusion, as she would put it. For once a delusion has you in its grip, there is no escape. Unaware, amidst the mass of lies, you begin to accept the least outrageous ones as truths and thus enter the realm of error, wandering into a thicket of self-deception that once trespassed is well nigh impossible to leave. And yet her savvy logic could not account for the fact that this tempest of emotion and its fantastic affect was undeniably real. It was a real delusion. And what was the difference between a real delusion and a healing mystical occurrence?

Before him stood the dome; the piping-hot water gushed from it directly into the icy winter air, producing a cloud of steam like exhaust from a train. His pulse quickened. He could feel the thirst. All the mystery, coincidence and peculiarity had not altered his commitment to drink. On the contrary, this had usurped all other commitments. Standing before the source was an old woman. She didn't smile, but went along with her task unaffected by his presence, her fragile, yet determined hands trembling as she held out a bottle to the water. Then, as she was returning her provision to her basket, she made eye contact with him. The two paused for a moment, as though in recognition of the change that had occurred. Whether she could see it or not, however, was of no concern; important was that he had finally realized the futility of resistance. She nodded and went on her way.

A decision based on life or death is made expediently and executed impulsively; but one that affects the direction of life is never made without hesitation. For during these moments we find ourselves confronted with choice: choice of an infinite nature, choice that offers neither advantage nor disadvantage. And just as we may choose in which country, province or city we wish to live, we may do likewise with career, status and lifestyle. In this sense, some of us realize our potential to travel without movement. And it can be argued that these are the true voyagers of our society. For travel has become too easy; and change of environment by no means necessitates change in spirit. The only way to achieve a voyage is by traveling within; and once we take on this arduous venture, we are faced with an overwhelming amount of choice—indeed, a penumbra of possibilities—that has utterly no affect on our natural state of being.

He closed his eyes, held the cup to his lips and prayed for a miracle; but resolution abided, and without regret or remorse he imbibed the transforming draft. His head became light, his eyes lost focus and, as the incalescent waves ran through him, he fell into a state of suspension. But the heat, instead of resting in his stomach, this time was building in his chest, consuming his lungs and besieging his heart, mixing with his blood, flowing throughout his being. Then it rose up his spine and burst into the back of his head in a euphoric rush, discharging in his mind and bringing him to a state of sheer ecstasy. All was color and blur, and he saw the entopic phenomena that occur during a migraine or an attack of light-headedness; tiny psychedelic curly worms and twinkling stars that danced in the peripheral vision, twirling and bobbing like strange little creatures that formed into whispering faces, appearing and vanishing in a sparkle of light.

He inhaled the steam, and then filled a second glass. Today demanded a potent dose if it was to quell this tumult of energy inside him, as if something was tearing his soul in two, and yet unable to release whatever was caged within. He drank again, and then another time, over and over until his stomach had been filled to capacity. Then he held out his hand and, stepping back into the steam, looked at it. But what he saw was beyond his wildest dreams.

Chapter XXXVI

Käfer's was magnificent. No less than three scandalously coifed tinkerbells were huddled around a businessman demanding that he kiss each one on the lips. Another dame, standing alone at the end of the bar with an empty martini glass before her, had placed the feather of a peacock in her cleavage. Even the piano-player looked three sheets to the wind as he dished out a sloppy, but heart-felt rendition of "Mack the Knife." Our favorite bureaucrat was there as well, aping into his imaginary microphone, stumbling over himself and blowing kisses to the Käfer-girls. The opera had finished, releasing a flood of tuxedoed denizens into the already crowded bar. The wooden propeller spun listlessly above it all, cutting the air that was saturated with the smoke of Cuban cigars, French perfume and the sweet smell of success. Yes, the holidays were over and Wiesbaden had regained its rhythm. The lipstick was thick, the dresses were tight and the heels were high. There were daringly cut suits and exotically trimmed facial hair. All around was money, jewelry and gold. And, ensphered by it all was our friend Jürgen.

He had arrived early—securing an excellent position at the bar: central, facing the entrance with speedy access to the toilets —and embraced the kinetic atmosphere by ordering himself a double scotch on the rocks. He couldn't help from smiling. Every time he did, some over-painted libertine who happened to intercept the glance promptly returned the gesture with interest. The surge was apparently a release owing to the end of holiday obligations. For these people, the oyster had come to taste better than gingerbread, champagne better than mulled wine. Nonetheless, Jürgen loved this atmosphere and wouldn't have it any other way. He toasted himself before sipping his scotch; and then looking at his watch, he noticed it was five past the hour, chuckling at the thought that Robert was late. He sipped his drink and looked out into the crowd.

It was around half past the hour when Jürgen began to wonder about his tardy friend. If Robert was nothing else in life, he was punctual. And contrary to his proclivity to the student lifestyle, he never took advantage of what we call here in Germany "The Academic Quarter"—those fifteen minutes of tardiness that is every student's right. This was distinctly unlike him. If it were anyone else, a half-hour of lateness wouldn't inspire any particular concern. But Jürgen knew something was amiss. He finished off his scotch and ordered another, wondering if his friend could be hurt or in danger; based on Robert's personality and Wiesbaden's crime rate, both possibilities seemed unlikely. The dilemma caught him completely off guard.

Three quarters of an hour passed with no sign of Jürgen's friend. The concern was plainly visible on his face. If Robert hadn't shown up by now, he wasn't going to. Suddenly Jürgen became aware of the noise and smoke. His head was dizzy from the alcohol. He looked over to the bartender, who had been watching him, and signaled for the bill. It was needless to wait any longer, but the weather outside was freezing cold—the temperatures had been terrible lately—and since the bar was at least warm, Jürgen decided to linger a bit more. Near him a

226

woman was laughing hysterically at her friend. The cackling was unbearable. The bartender returned and Jürgen offered a generous tip; but before he could pay, the bartender explained that the drinks were on the house. Jürgen was too tired to question the matter. He just wanted to leave. And then, as if the bartender's behavior wasn't already odd, he reminded Jürgen to "never miss a week" and told him to "sleep it all off." It didn't make sense that Robert would take off on a whim. He rarely left Wiesbaden. Most Germans spend half their lives on the autobahn; Robert didn't even own a car! The bartender was watching Jürgen as he sat there hesitating to leave.

It's difficult to recall precisely what happened at this point; however, as Jürgen would recount the story in years to come, the bartender made a curious twist of the head as if to look at something behind him. Regardless of what really happened, Jürgen's glance followed and found itself fixed on an object leaning in the corner of the bar. He took off his glasses, cleaned them with his shirtsleeve and looked again. It took a few moments to focus on what he was staring at. Yes, he had seen this object before—long, thin and black with a particular handle on top, a handle made of ivory in the shape of an Egyptian sarcophagus; a cane...the cane! The cane of an eccentric old man whose presence had been felt, and yet who had been conspicuously absent from his favorite meeting point. The vision was accompanied by an extraordinary thought. And all of a sudden his fears vanished. He knew exactly where his friend had gone. Only no one would believe him.

Chapter XXXVII

Jürgen was the first to discover. Nevertheless, contrary to his instinctual impulse to inform the world, he kept the event to himself, shrouding it in secrecy, treating it as a stealth agreement, like a pact without a partner. After receiving what he later called his "message from beyond," he was convinced his friend needed him more than ever. The crisis called for action, and thus he took it upon himself to cover up the event that nobody knew about. He fibbed to Petra about the Thursday night meeting, adding that Robert sent his greetings, and went as far as to phone the guest family whose attic Robert had occupied during the past four and a half months. He told them that Robert was on holiday and not to worry about their guest's absence. They had no idea he had been gone to begin with and went on to explain they had been concerned for some time; they rarely saw him and remarked that he periodically spent entire days locked up in his room. He never came downstairs to visit, and yet there was evidence that he went through their things when they were away. On one day in particular, he was fiddling with their clock and didn't even bother to put it back. Mr. Bornheimer (Robert had never mentioned their name) said that he and his wife went up to his room to see what was the matter and caught him hiding in the closet, shivering like a leaf, but they were ashamed to confront the poor man having so been cornered. Apart from this incident, no sounds came from his room; no friends came by to see him and only once in a while he would receive calls. They were concerned for his health. Jürgen was sympathetic to these concerns, but opted nonetheless to follow his hunch that his friend was all right.

At first Petra dealt with the situation in her usual pragmatic fashion. When Jürgen, however, broke down one evening, admitting that he had lied and sharing his experience at Käfer's, she forgave him for the fib, but found anything to do with that "pseudo-scientific windbag" suspicious. She was skeptical as to the likelihood that a cane would be purposely left in the back of a bar, and the idea that the bartender was in on it was poppycock. She attempted to analyze the action based on what she had learned of Robert's philosophy. She saw him as the type who possessed what she called a "stringently open mind." This peculiar quality, coupled with an inherent confusion regarding his environment, produced a worldview that could only be described as enigmatic. As far as she knew him, the possibilities were endless. Perhaps the immersion in the new culture had impacted him to a degree that he lost his connection with reality. His overexerted brain had likely surpassed its carrying capacity for new cultural information, ergo reaching a critical breaking point, causing him to retreat to a more philosophically familiar environment. In simple terms, Germany was too much for him. He was probably at that moment in a hotel near the Frankfurt International Airport, watching American TV and deciding whether or not to buy a ticket home.

But Robert wasn't at the airport; and as time passed, Petra's theories aged and weakened, losing their youthful confidence. Robert would have eventually come back, or at least written. At one point she broke down and entertained Jürgen's notion that his friend had somehow fallen "into the mystic." Luckily, she came to her senses and dismissed the thought as a psychic manifestation of her mourning his loss. In any case, she was impressed by Jürgen's resolve. He obviously missed his friend, but showed absolutely no worry toward his whereabouts. In fact, he spoke of him as though he were still around. Sometimes he would say he was going to visit Robert. A few hours would pass and he would return, distant, and yet rejuvenated.

The strongest argument Jürgen had in his favor was the coincidental absence of the Grand Pooh-Bah of dreamers and flakes. But as far as Petra was concerned, that doddering kook could have been straitjacketed by now. Anyone could see the old dip wasn't playing with a full deck, and all his talk of alchemistic hoodoo-voodoo and Masonic mumbo-jumbo never helped Robert or Jürgen to keep a grip on reality to begin with. One must be half-delirious to go for such baloney. Simply put, he's a quack. She focused on helping Robert in the way she knew best: the practical. After all, human beings don't just disappear. They flee, they escape, they're kidnapped, they're murdered, they die; but they do not disappear. Dead or alive, the body is found somewhere...at least for a time. She was the only one to think of contacting Robert's family in America and of going to the Department of Missing Persons. She worked hard on it because, like Jürgen, she missed him.

Chapter XXXVIII

On the day she came home from her holidays (at the same time Petra was arriving at the police station, where already from a distance, she could see the officer at the reception desk was in a bad mood) Monika entered her apartment building to find an un-posted letter in the mailbox. Robert had left her. She made herself a coffee, laid back in her couch and looked up at the palm fronds, reading the letter over and again. His words seemed distant, desperate, and yet fixed on his decision to leave. She tried to understand what drove him away, even entertained the idea that his intentions were singular, and once having achieved his carnal objective, he no longer wanted her. She broke down one night, sick of her life and all the fleeting affairs, wishing she were a girl again. She crumpled up the letter, threw it against the wall, and cried.

That was the beginning. As time went on, however, her anger subsided into frustration, and later into concern. Maybe he was sick of life as well, and also hated being an adult. She reread the letter yet another time and the words sounded less distant. He was not so unlike herself and for that she couldn't hate him. For as much as she wanted his body, she also wanted his company. This is what hurt: his laugh that came against efforts to keep his composure, his winsome moods and boyish smile that appeared when he saw her. This is what filled her chest with a cloud of pain.

One evening she found herself at the Philharmonie—alone. She ordered a Calvados and thought of him. In a way, she realized he hadn't left her at all. Not in the way he went. After all, it was she who said that he was from "someplace else"; and it was that instability, that brewing desire for change, which made him attractive. She remembered flirting with him and the simple pleasures of getting to know another human being, and in this case quite a special one. It was like aiding a wounded animal that would surely run as soon as it was cured. And yet he was just what she needed. For without knowing it, her supporting his desire for change was curing her own frustrations with stability and stagnation. It's a funny occurrence that our problems are often solved when we're thinking about them least, when we're helping someone out. The last sip of Calvados went down smoothly, and she couldn't help from smiling at the thought of that confused, hopeful letter. It was the beginning of a ritual that lasted for years. In the end she missed him too. She missed him like someone who had died.

Chapter XXXIX

The following is Robert's letter to Monika, the last time she would ever hear from him:

Dear Monika,

By the time you receive this letter, I'll be gone. I realize your feelings will be hurt, and what I ask of you will seem unfair. To where I'm going, there can be no return. There will be no address where I can be reached and no telephone where my voice can be heard. And once I've made this step, I'll be unable to contact you or anyone else. It has been advised that I cut my ties immediately, but I must make this final contact. I can't leave without saying goodbye.

I'm faced with a great decision: one that I can't reveal, and yet is influenced nonetheless by you. For some time I've recognized in myself a desire to separate the elements of my person, the various parts, which together constitute what some would call the soul. Perhaps it's only an act of self-assessment; and yet, in another sense, I suspect these feelings touch the mystic. I know this sounds strange, and I understand that I'm playing with my sanity, but I can no longer ignore the magic that life has been casting around me. Don't you see? I'm failing in the world of the practical. That's to say the world that has been collapsing around me ever since our coincidental meeting at the Café Parsival.

I hope you understand why I couldn't go back to my life at home, and why I cannot return to the one I've started here. I must push on, further, into the unknown. I suspect it's all we can do. For years, I've asked myself why fight it. But until now, I've yet to actually act upon this realization. This time I'm going to follow my heart, and if it leads me away from everything I've been taught, then so be it. I admit I'm scared. But at the same time, I'm happy to be acting on a decision. This is that moment of joyous resolution before we pull the trigger.

I've somehow met myself: a weird projection of my future. And now I'm becoming the old man before me! My thoughts are affecting a metamorphosis, a powerful, burning pain. And I don't know why, but it's linked to the water. Something is driving me to pursue this mystery to its end. I must know what they call perfect enlightenment. And thus I follow them, regardless of what they present me. Regardless if it's true or a vicious lie, I must drink what they offer.

Once you made the joke that you were here for the water. I've come to believe it has brought me here as well. I believe it has brought us all here. And as crazy as this may sound, I want you to know that this is where I am. From this moment onward, there is no place else where you can be closer to me. If it's not asking too much, please think of me from time to time.

I'll be thinking of you. My actions have frozen me in time, and for that you'll always be near my heart.

Robert

Two days later Robert Holsen was found dead in the forest, along the path called Philosopher's Way, not far from the Russian chapel. A woman walking her dog found the corpse, barely clothed and anemic, nestled among some bushes and snow. At first the police didn't know what to do with the body; there was no identification on it, and no one in Wiesbaden to claim it. It wasn't until the Department of Missing Persons intervened that the mystery was solved for the few who knew him. The autopsy revealed that at the time of death the victim was saturated with lithium, sulfate, bromide and arsenic. In addition, bichloride of mercury was found in the tissue alluding to foul play. Blood analysis proved that from the potent mineral waters he was ingesting eleven times the recommended dosage. He had reached a state of delirium where he didn't notice the dropping temperature and simply froze to death. Nevertheless the doctors were perplexed. The warning signs must have been as plain as day. Intense migraine headaches, shortness of breath, nausea and aching kidneys were common complaints from patients who drank too much of the hot metallic waters. And yet the tragedy could not have been haphazard; it was evident by the positioning of the head against a tree that the young man had carefully chosen his final place of rest. The hands were bent in a peculiar fashion; one was open, strangely sacrificial, as if to receive an angel's embrace. The other was grasping an empty cup. The police made jokes about the foolish smiling face.